I0557330

LIES UNSEEN

LIES UNSEEN
BY MARK WRIGHT

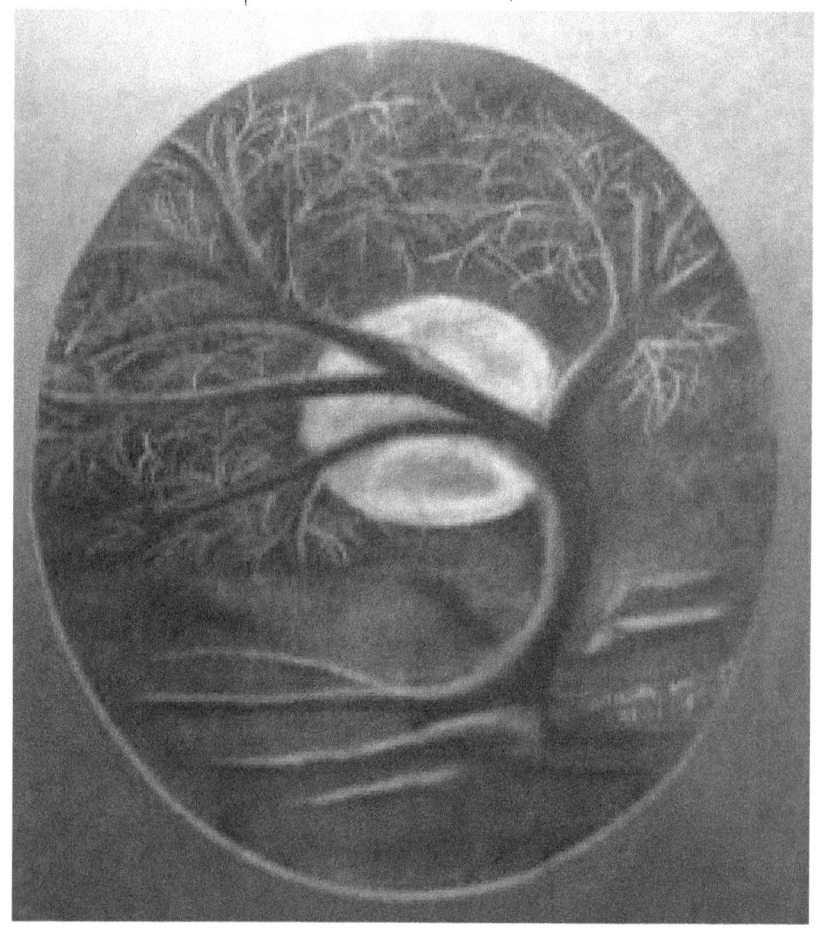

LIES UNSEEN – MARK WRIGHT

Publisher books are published by

Special book excerpts or customized printings can also be created to fit specific needs. For details write or phone the office of the publisher.

KDP (KINDLE DIRECT PUBLISHING) SELF PUBLISHING

Edited by Lorraine Wright

Cover and interior design by Mark Wright

Paperback ISBN-979-8-218-54370-9
ebook ISBN- 979-8-218-54369-3

Manufactured in the United States of America

First Edition October 2024

To my wife,

Thank you for all your love and support in all areas of my life. Your help in writing this book and offering ideas was especially appreciated and needed. I look forward to the future of our adventures in the next chapter of these characters lives.

Love, Mark

Acknowledgements:

To Lorraine for your help with editing and assisting in creation of this book.

Author's Note

The information within this book is purely fictional. The characters and situations do not exist, nor did they happen. However, this book includes elements that may not be suitable for all readers. People with childhood trauma, abuse, and/or Post Traumatic Stress Disorder may be negatively affected. Readers who may be sensitive to these elements please take note.

Introduction

Lies Unseen

A story that reveals the hidden secrets of family violence and its origins. How it can be visible to everyone, and no one sees it. As a young boy trapped in this world our main character systematically develops a series of secrets to reveal the truth.

Contents

HALF TITLE
TITLE PAGE
COPYWRIGHT PAGE
DEDICATION AND ACKNOWLEDGEMENT
AUTHOR NOTE
INTRODUCTION
TABLE OF CONTENTS

CHAPTER 1-THE TREASURE TROVE................- 8 -

CHAPTER 2 - HELP ....- 25 -

CHAPTER 3- THE STORY BEGINS..................- 51 -

CHAPTER 4- IS IT WILLY ....- 66 -

CHAPTER 5- A CLOSER LOOK ....- 76 -

CHAPTER 6- NEW HOPE ....- 97 -

CHAPTER 7-A TRUTH REVEALED................- 121 -

CHAPTER 8- DIRTY LITTLE SECRETS ....- 143 -

CHAPTER 9- THE TRUTH ....- 161 -

CHAPTER 10- FARMER MILES ....- 174 -

CHAPTER 11- AS TIME GOES ON ....- 197 -

CHAPTER 12- THE SURPRISE.......................- 208 -

PREFACE
ABOUT AUTHOR

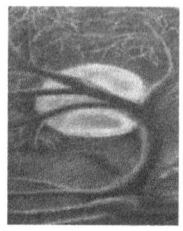

CHAPTER 1-THE TREASURE TROVE

"Come on, let's go down to the river" Willy said. "Dad says not to. He says there are snakes and other varmints, and we could get bit" said Miles. Willy looks up and smiles "don't be afraid, we won't go that far down. Just to the first ledge so we can explore the woods." "I am not afraid. I just don't want to get in trouble. My butt still hurts from the last time" Miles said. "Come on Miles, just for a little while" Willy said. "Fine" Miles said. They took off running towards the edge of the woods where the river was located.

The woods surround a trailer park, where they live, and hide it from their neighbors. The trailer homes around them are run down, with trash in the yards, and cars on blocks, most of which have been sitting there forever. The mobile homes themselves are old and literally falling apart. One trailer has a whole exterior wall fallen off and the owner used cardboard and duct tape to replace it. The neighbors are rarely seen outside, and when they are, they look as worn out and decrepit as their homes.

Miles and Willy are stepbrothers that are the same age, ten years old, and they love to explore. Especially in places that are forbidden. As they approach the edge of the woods, Willy slows down and looks back.

Miles, although taller than Willy, is a much slower runner. Willy stops to wait for his brother to catch up. "Let's go down over here where there is a trail." As they walk over and enter the wooded area, they can feel a major change in the temperature.

Walking down the trail, they could see a whole world of new things appear right before their eyes. No more dead grass and dirt patches. No more old run-down homes or cars. There were trees as far as their eyes could see. They could see flowers and other foliage with bright colors growing all throughout the riverbed. At the bottom of the hill was a creek, only a few feet wide, flowing back to the left. Rocks and tree limbs of all sizes appear as steps, as they make their way down to the bottom of the riverbed. Miles is always amazed whenever he enters the forest and sees all the beauty and wonder displayed each time. Sometimes he wishes he could live down here forever, away from all the dirt and nasty things of the world.

Miles said "Hey, we are not going into the water, are we?" "Why not?" Willy asked as he continued walking down the trail. Suddenly he stopped, looked to his right and said "Oh my God! Look at that, it's a bike! Someone left a bike down here!" "No way" Miles said looking totally surprised. "Holy cow! Look over there; it's a Jumbo Jack dump truck with controls!" This was better than any

Christmas they've ever had thought the boys. A big screen TV, a laptop, tires from a car, and more! A whole treasure trove of stuff, some of which they had wished for, but never received.

Things that only people with money could have. Here are all of these treasures just tossed out into the woods, all along the riverbed. They inched their way up the creek to their treasure trove. As Miles worked his way towards the dump truck, he could see a small fish swimming in the creek below. He stopped and watched the fish as if mesmerized by its freedom. Miles jumped across the small creek and landed on a large rock, skidding off the rock's other side in his hurry to reach the dump truck. "Oops" he said.

The first thing Willy pulls out is the bike. A Mongoose fat tire, mountain bike. It was blue and had extra-long handlebars. One of the best bikes ever made Willy thought. Even the brakes were attached to the handlebars. "Hey Miles come over here and look at this!" Willy hollered. By this time Miles was on the other side of the creek and had reached the Jumbo Jack dump truck. He was in the process of pulling it out from under the brush. It was big enough for him to ride on! He had never seen one of these in real life, only in the magazines in his school's library.

The dump truck was yellow in color, with really big stickers on the side of the truck that said, 'Jumbo Jack'. Black stripes ran along the bucket on the rear of the back cover. As Miles looked it over, he realized it was electric. He opened the back and saw that the battery was disconnected. He connected it together and the dash lit up! He climbed up onto the seat, turned the key, and pulled back on the lift arm that lifted the bucket up in the air. The bucket went straight up and almost caused him to lose his balance and fall off. He lowered the bucket and looked over at Willy in total amazement!

Willy was standing, scratching the back of his head. "I don't get it Miles, why would anyone throw away a perfectly good bike like this?" Miles said "Yeah, look at this dump truck, not a scratch on it and it works!" "Oh man, we need to get this stuff out of this creek bed before someone else finds it, take it home, and hide it there" Willy said. Looking confused, Miles says "Um…no. Dad said to stay away from this creek. If we take this stuff home, they are going to know we were here. I don't need my ass whupped again. We can hide this stuff down here and not say anything." Willy just stared at Miles not sure what to think as he looked around and realized they hadn't even gone through all the stuff yet. Even the big screen TV had a new price tag on it and didn't even look as if it had been used at all.

Suddenly, they were startled by Jimmy screaming their names. "Willy…Miles…where are you? I saw you coming this way and know you're down there! Don't try to hide from me! I will find you!" Jimmy screamed. The boys quickly ducked down to not be seen by Jimmy. "Oh shit!" Willy whispered. Jimmy was Miles's second, oldest brother and he was a real brat! Always watching over their shoulders and tattling on them, getting them into trouble!

"Oh man Willy, we cannot let Jimmy see this stuff! He will get us into a whole lot of trouble!" Miles whispered. "What do we do?" Willy asked. Miles said "hide this stuff under the bushes as far as you can. Then you run that way and come up to the top of the riverbed on that side and I will go to the other side and come up way over there" pointing the opposite direction. "That way he doesn't know where we were at."

Willy shook his head and pushed the bike over to hide it under a bush. Crouching down, he started moving towards the area that Miles had pointed to. Miles pushed the dump truck out of sight and took off the other way. Immeasurable fear rose up inside each of these boys. If their mom ever finds out they are here, she will punish them in ways that cannot be imagined, just for playing here and being curious, adventurous boys!

Once they both reached the area Miles had pointed to, they ran up the hill, coming out at the top in separate places. However, Willy stopped just as Miles came out of the woods. He saw his mom with Jimmy, holding her whip. He knew what that meant. Willy braced himself for another bad day, shaking and quivering with fear, dreading what he knew would come next.

Suddenly, Miles topped the hill, coming to a stop. "Oh shit" he said! "I told you! I told you they were down here!" Jimmy screamed, jumping up and down, pointing at Miles. Miles knew what this meant. His heart felt like it was going to bounce right out of his chest. "Where is your brother?" his stepmother said.

Miles just stood there, staring at her, not saying a word. He was frozen with fear and knew that he would be beaten once again for whatever reason she deemed worthy of a beaten. As Jimmy and their mother continued to approach, Jimmy seemed so excited because he knew what was coming. "Mom, you want me to hold him down for you?" Jimmy asked. "No. He knows what will happen if he runs. I am going to ask you again, where is your damn brother, where is Willy?" Miles gulped and said "I don't know. He ran off when he heard Jimmy calling for us earlier. I don't know which way he went."

"He's lying!" Jimmy said. "Jimmy, go down there and get your brother! I don't want to have to do this twice! You boys were told by your father not to come down here! How is it that a boy that is so smart in school can be so stupid?" Mom said. "I don't know" Miles said as tears welled up in his eyes, anticipating the thrashing he was about to get. Under his breath he said, "run Willy, get away, I can handle this."

Jimmy took off and went down the side of the hill, while Miles stood trembling with fear. A short time later Jimmy came back up, dragging Willy by one of his legs, kicking and screaming. "Let go of me you son of a bitch! Let go of me!" Willy screamed, kicking and twisting, trying to escape. Jimmy was laughing out loud, feeling proud of himself. He hung on tight; making sure Willy could not get away, thinking once again he had caught his prey. Jimmy and Willy slowly moved towards the tree Mom was standing under, delivering him to his mother at the top of the hill was his satisfaction. Mom had a smile on her face, anticipating giving Willy his punishment.

Miles watched, thinking Willy was being treated like an animal, captured, and dragged to its death. He wanted to save his stepbrother from the harm that was about to begin, but he realized that Jimmy and his stepmother were far too big to fight. He could not overpower them. His stepmother was just plain ass mean, and if he tried to stop her punishing Willy, he would only find himself being punished even worse!

As Jimmy drug Willy across the field, Miles realized he had to save himself. His mom was just standing there watching and smiling, looking evil. She lit up a cigarette, took a long drag and blew the smoke out slowly, as if giving herself a reward. She looked over at Miles and said "you will never see the light of day again, neither of you! I will lock you up so tight, you won't even get chance to even think about doing what you are told not to do! Jimmy, bring that boy over here and tie his ass to that tree!" Mom said.

Miles stood there wondering were we stupid or what? We knew what would happen if we were caught. Yet here we are once again playing the odds and losing. Just last night we were told by our father not to come down here and yet we did it anyway. Thinking they would not be caught and could outsmart their mom and Jimmy. They are just boys being boys, loving to explore Miles thought.

Miles watched as Jimmy pulled Willy to the one lone tree that stood outside of the forest. A tree Miles and Willy were well acquainted with. Mom turned and looked at Miles and said, "get your pants down now and get up against that tree!" Miles just stared at his stepmother. She screamed "NOW!"

Something cracked inside of Miles. He snapped. Suddenly he looked up at her with pure hatred. Knowing he would regret the next thing he was about to do, but before he could stop himself, words shot out of his mouth "fuck this!" Off he ran down into the creek bed, running as fast as he could into the woods like a panther, screaming "I am so sorry Willy!" To his surprise he heard Willy scream back, "run Miles, get as far away as you can!"

Miles knew Jimmy was too slow to catch him, but he still didn't dare stop running. So, he had to run as fast as he could run. He had to get to the bottom of the creek and follow it as far as it would go. So down to the bottom he went, heading out away from the trailer park to an unknown place. As he took off, he heard his stepmother scream, "go get him Jimmy! That little asshole is running!"

By the time Jimmy had finished tying Willy to the tree and started running towards the woods, Miles had already reached the bottom of the creek. Although Miles had never been past the trailer park in the creek bed, he hoped the creek would take him out away from the trailer park far enough so Jimmy wouldn't catch him. Jumping tree roots, rocks, and weeds; falling in muddy holes, getting back up, Miles kept running. Not ever stopping to look back. At some point he could no longer hear Willy's screams. He also could no longer hear Jimmy's footsteps. Not willing to take a chance, he kept running. The creek began to disappear until it was just woods and weeds. As night began to fall over the horizon, he realized he had the advantage.

Darkness allowed Miles to slow down and plan out his next moves. Taking a deep breath, he felt like he might be safe...for now. Miles knew that Jimmy was a wimp who afraid of the dark. Which brought him to his second thought, how can a boy as big as Jimmy be afraid of the dark? Oh well, he thought, that played out in his favor.

As he continued to run, his mind began to wonder back to the trailer park. He wondered about what was happening to poor Willy. Miles felt really bad that he left his stepbrother behind to face the cruelty he knew Jimmy and his stepmother would dish out. Knowing his stepmother's desire to cause as much harm as much as possible, he wished there could have been another way. He often felt like it was his responsibility to protect Willy because of his size. "God...why did I have to leave Willy? I'm nothing but a rotten wimp to leave him there! I should just suck it up and go get him" Miles said to himself knowing he could not do it.

Willy was a small boy compared to Miles. Even though they were the same age, Willy had not hit his growth spurt yet. He was only about four feet tall with brown hair that Mom chopped up with her scissors, especially his last haircut. He had a small face with brown eyes and really big ears. His shoulders were stocky, and his legs were much thicker than Miles's legs. He could run much faster than Miles, as well as most of the kids his age, even though his legs were shorter.

Miles just kept getting taller. At ten years old, he was just above five feet tall. His hair was red, and his eyes were blue with a face full of freckles. He had a tall skinny body with long legs. But just like Willy, Miles's hair was chopped up. Although Miles was not very fast, he could outrun Jimmy, and right now, that was all that mattered.

As Miles ran, he began to try to think of ways to help Willy. He was beginning to feel a lot of guilt for leaving him at home alone; knowing the pain and humiliation Willy was probably feeling. However, this was something the two of them had talked about a lot.

If ever there was a situation where they both were in trouble, they both agreed that they would try to get the hell out of there and not come back. Even if it meant only one of them could get away. Miles knew this was what he wanted Willy to do. He didn't understand why he didn't run. He also knew that at this point if, he got caught now, he would suffer a fate worse than death.

All Miles knew was that ever since his dad, Robert Dingwald, married his step-mother (Marilyn) and they moved here, his life was a living hell. He had to constantly watch over his shoulder to make sure she wasn't watching or that Jimmy wasn't standing in the background, trying to get him into trouble.

Miles's memory of his biological Mother was very little. He had been told by Lewis, his older brother, and the family that his real Mother had been diagnosed with cancer and had passed away a few years back. His Father was not as involved in their children as she was. Miles believed he married his stepmother because he was looking for someone to take care of his children.

The stepmother scared Miles to death. She was constantly looking for reasons to punish him. Sometimes her punishments were so harsh; they left extremely thick scars on Miles's body. He hated the shed the most of all. Being locked in there, with no clothes on, and unable to see truly scared him. Bugs crawling all over his body! It was really hot in there during the summer!

She seemed to like Jimmy because he didn't get punished as much because he kissed her ass, did everything she asked him to and that's what she liked. Miles couldn't seem to make himself do the stuff his stepmother wanted him to. Miles thought he was hardheaded because he just could not let her have her way and give her his soul! No matter what...he would fight to be himself!

Miles's real family consisted of Lewis who was fourteen, Jimmy who was twelve, and his younger sister, Carolyn who is only nine. They very seldom interacted with their father. Miles did not fully grasp what his father did most of the time, although he knew that his father drank a lot of alcohol.

As they grew up, he and his siblings were passed around to other family members when they were younger.

Miles liked it when they all lived at Mama and Papa's (his grandparent's house. It was not as chaotic all the time and they knew the rules. They each had their own lives and friends. Even though Jimmy has always been a brat, he wasn't nearly as bad as he is now. But when Papa put his foot down, everyone knew what to do.

To keep from having to watch over the smaller children, Marilyn, his stepmother, would draw a circle on a wall with chalk and make Miles, Willy, and/or Carolyn sit in chairs in front of the circle and place their nose on the wall in the chalked circle. She would threaten them, if they rubbed off any of the chalk, that she would give them ten lashes per each discretion! They knew she meant it! Right next to them was the whip she threatened to use.

Marilyn had two children. Rebecca at fourteen was the oldest and Willy was ten. Rebecca is like her mother, plain ass mean.

Dad once told all of them that if they got good grades on their report cards, they could stay up and watch TV late with him. Miles came home with straight A's as always. He laid his report card on the counter with the others. Rebecca picked it up and tore it into pieces. She started screaming at Miles and ran over and grabbed him by the throat. She picked him up by his throat, lifted him up into the air, and started screaming at him.

"You think you are better than the rest of us, you fucking pig! I hate you and I wish my mom had never met you people! I am going to choke the life out of you motherfucker." Miles was swinging his arms and trying to kick her to get her to let him go. All the sudden Lewis came running across the room and tackled her, knocking Miles away. Lewis screamed at her "stop it you crazy bitch, that's my brother your hurting!"

Later that day when their stepmother came home, Rebecca lied to her and told her Lewis had attacked her. Marilyn grabbed Lewis by the ear and forced him out to the shed.

Inside the shed was a spike that was driven deep into the ground. Welded to the spike was a chain about four feet long. At the other end of the chain was a shackle. The shed itself was a six foot by eight-foot metal building that was placed onto a concrete pad. Inside the shed on the walls and door were bloody handprints and finger marks. These were made by kids that were locked in there and indicated that they were trying to find a way out.

She used the shed as a punishment tool when she felt one of the children needed extra punishment. Miles and Willy were frequent targets. Today, she had Lewis in the shed. She would have him strip off all his clothes, even his underwear! Then she would shut the door and lock it, leaving him in the shed until his dad got home, or until she chose to let him out.

Miles and Willy had been inside this hot box shed many times. The shackle itself rubbed the skin off their ankles, causing major sores for days and they had permanent scars too. As Lewis was being forced into the shed, Miles screamed at his stepmother and told her Rebecca was a liar. "She attacked me" Miles said. "She tried to choke me to death and Lewis was protecting me. Rebecca tore up my report card and threw it away because I made straight A's" he explained. The stepmother looked at Miles with a grin and said "well then, this should be a reminder to you of what happens when you think you are better than the rest of us! Maybe you should quit trying to be such a smartass!" she said.

"You want to go into the shed too boy?" she asked. "No" Miles said. She pushed Lewis into the shed and shackled his ankle. As she stepped back out of the shed, she said. "Just wait until your dad gets home! He is going to whup the fuck out of you!" "You will never touch my daughter again!" she exclaimed.

Miles felt like he was broken. He loved his brother and never wanted to be the cause of him getting into trouble. As much as he wanted to sacrifice himself for his brother, he knew Lewis would be mad at him if he did. He knew how this was going to play out. Lewis was going to be angry at him, even though he did nothing wrong. Although inside of himself, Miles felt like he was the cause of Lewis's punishment.

Miles often wondered how he was supposed to not be smart, when he was smart. He couldn't help getting good grades. It was not his fault that others were less intelligent than he was. They were constantly targeting him because of his ability to make good grades in school. Now because of his latest straight A's report card, they were attacking again, and Lewis was being punished because of protecting Miles.

Later tonight when dad got home, Marilyn revealed that Lewis had done something she believed required more punishment. The rest of the children left and went out into the fields because they knew it was going to be very loud, and Lewis would not be able to walk when they were done punishing him.

Their Dad (Robert Dingwald) was a daily alcohol drinker, normally to excess. Hopefully, today would be one of those days when he couldn't make it up the driveway. If so, Lewis would have to go down the street and get him and his car. Their dad was a short man, about five foot two, with brown hair and brown eyes. He had a large, red nose and tiny lips. His face looked somewhat crooked most of the time. He had stocky shoulders with a big belly. He walked with his toes pointed outwards, like a rodeo cowboy. When he got angry, he would tear off his belt and start swinging, not caring who or what he hit.

All his children knew not to fight back, because when he was in this mood, it would be a lot worse if they fought back and tried to defend themselves. Sometimes it seemed like the stepmother was looking for reasons to have him beat one of the kids. Mostly, Miles and Willy were her biggest targets.

Miles wished his dad didn't drink so much, maybe then he would see what was happening. Miles remembered that night because he knew what was going to happen to Lewis. He wished he could stop it, but when he tried to stop it in the past, it just made matters worse. Although Miles thought that if he could just change himself completely, then maybe she would stop targeting him. It would be like giving his soul to the devil though and he refused to do that. That would mean Marilyn won and he just couldn't let her win over him.

The last time when Willy was in trouble, he told his father what really happened. His father got so mad, he grabbed Miles by the throat and shoved him into a wall! Telling him to shut his mouth and leave things alone! Miles often wondered why his family hated the truth or him so much.

Miles realized that he had been running all this time, not paying attention. He also realized that too much thinking about this caused him anguish. He looked around at his current location and found that he had made it to the road. Since the road traveled both directions, he needed to decide where he wanted to end up, where he was going. He was getting hungry, and since the night had fallen over the horizon, he found that it was hard to see his way in the woods. He believed that he had left Jimmy way behind.

He also believed that his family would not come looking for him. Instead, they would just go on as if he never existed. If he went to the right, it would take him into town. Although he was not very well known in this town. He was quite certain that someone would turn him into the police if they found him alone outside. If he went to the left, it would be into a completely unknown area. He had no idea what he would run into going in that direction.

At the same time, he thought about Willy and wondered how he was doing. What had they actually done to him and wondered if he should go back and try to save Willy.

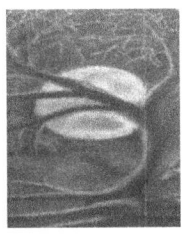

CHAPTER 2 - HELP

Miles stopped and thought holy shit! I cannot believe this! Apple trees, hundreds of them across the street, full of apples! Dinner is served! Miles snuck across the road to the fencing where the trees were at. He noticed the fence was an electric, barbed wire fence. He could hear the buzzing of the electricity, so he knew it had power to it. This was something that he had learned from his grandpa. He wormed his way around the fencing by pulling his shirt sleeves over his hands to protect them. Then he pushed the fence down with his foot. This kept him from being electrified. Then he climbed through to the apple trees.

He started picking apples to eat. "Oh man, I am so hungry!" he said out loud. As he ate, he was surrounded by apple trees, thinking how lucky he was these trees were here. He sat down on the ground next to one of the trees and finished eating the handful of apples that he had picked. He looked up and remembered something that his grandma had told him previously. Always give thanks to the things that feed you. "Thanks Mr. Tree" he said.

As Miles sat next to this tree, his mind began to trail off into his dream world. The only way he has ever been ever able to fall asleep was when he went into his imagination dream world. Due to his situation, his previous dream of escaping was showing signs of coming true. For a long time, he would lay in his bed at night and dream about how he planned to escape. His dream included each step that it would take to make his escape dream come true. However, as it turned out, Miles believed that dreams were not as easy to come true in real life as they were in his dream world. As he looked around at where he was at and how he got there, his eyes began to close. He was so sleepy after eating his apples that he fell asleep.

"Hey, get up boy!" a voice said poking Miles with a stick. "Get up! What are you doing here? Stealing my apples! Get up!" Miles opened his eyes and pushed the stick away from him. "Stop it!" Miles said. "That hurts!"

"It's supposed to hurt boy, wake your ass up! Why are you out here in my apple orchard?" the man asked. Miles looked up and he saw an old man standing over him. He had gray hair and bright blue eyes. His big ears were sticking out from under his round, straw hat. He was wearing blue jean coveralls and had some tools hanging from his side, a hammer and a tape measure. He was really tall or at least he looked tall thought Miles, looking up from the ground. Miles stood up and looked up...yep, this old man was really tall. Like the jolly green giant, only not green.

Miles spoke, "I am sorry, I wasn't trying to steal your apples, but I was hungry. I only ate a couple." "A couple? There is a whole pile of the mall the way back over there!" the old man said. Miles looked back and thought, oh man...I must have been really hungry!

"I'm sorry sir. I did not mean any harm. I was just passing through and was hungry. I don't have any money to pay you. I can work it off if you want?" Miles said. "You're fine" a female voice in the background said. Miles recognized that voice. It was his teacher, Mrs. Robinson. She was his favorite teacher and was always so nice to him. "He was just messing with you. I told him you were one of my students. Now what are you doing here and why are you sleeping in our field?"

Miles looked over at both Mr. and Mrs. Robinson and was not certain that sharing his reasons at this time was a good idea. So, he said "well, we had some issues at my house yesterday and I had to leave for a while. I didn't plan to stay here long. I just stopped here when I saw all these apples. I was so hungry! I ate them and I guess I just fell asleep. I will just get my stuff and get going" he said.

Mrs. Robinson looked over at Miles and said "we don't mind you being here child. We just want to know why you are. What happened that you felt like you had to leave your home?"

Mrs. Robinson was a tall, skinny woman. She had long, gray hair that ran down her back and her eyes were almost solid green. At school, she would put her hair up on top of her head in a big ball. Miles always wondered how she got all her hair to stay up there all day.

She was one of the older teachers in his school and everyone loved and respected her. She was always smiling, and she seemed to be happy all of the time.

"So, what's the plan here Pa?" she said. Pa looked up and said "young man, we need to get back to our house. Why don't you come with us, and we can sort this out?" Miles looked up and said "if it's all the same to you Mr. Robinson, I think I should just be on my way. I really don't want to cause you any more trouble, and I am sorry for eating so many of your apples. I guess I did not realize how hungry I was."

"What if you came home with us?" Mrs. Robinson said. "It is almost lunch time, and I can make us something to eat. Then you can sit down with us and maybe tell us more about your story and why you felt you had to leave your home. Once we have eaten, you can decide if you still want to leave us. Would that be okay?" "Yeah, I guess so" Miles responded. As they were walking, Mr. Robinson looked back and said "also, no one calls me Mr. Robinson. Pa will be just fine." "Yes sir, my name is Miles and you can call me Miles" Miles said trying to present a favorable, mature picture of himself.

They all turned and started walking towards the road where their truck was parked. As they approached the road, Miles stopped, not paying any attention to the fact that he was speaking out loud "oh wow, a Ford Model TT! What year? This is so cool!" Pa looked up and grinned.

"Know your trucks do you? Second one off the assembly line, my great granddaddy bought this one in 1917. This truck has been passed down through the years to family members. We were lucky enough to get the farm, so we got the truck." "Wow, this is so cool!" Miles said. "I've only read about them and have never really seen one of these type trucks! Honestly, didn't know they still existed except for in car shows. I have never been to a car show though. I always wanted to go to one. Does it have the original engine and transmission? I read somewhere that it is important. The tires don't look original, did you change them?" Miles smiled as his eyes lit up. He was so excited, he completely forgot about all of what got him here to begin with.

This truck was old! You can tell by the rust that was running all around the top and across the sides. The hood was slightly crooked and it had only one mirror on the passenger side of the truck. At the rear was the tailgate, which was hanging down and unlatched. Miles noticed the chains that should have been used to latch the tailgate were broken off. In the truck bed are wooden slats that run the full length of the bed.

His excitement showed both Ma and Pa that he was still a young boy. They could see his eyes light up as he was talking about this truck. Ma wondered what could have happened to him to make him want to just get up and leave his home and family. At school, he was such a quiet, intelligent boy. She was his Math and English teacher. He was one of the few students she had that didn't really require allot of attention. From talking to other teachers, he was a straight "A" student in their classes too. Some of the teachers said they felt like he believed he was smarter than they were. But not her. She knew he did not feel this way towards others and tried to defend him whenever this came up in conversations.

Pa looked over and said "I am glad you like my truck. I have enjoyed it for many years and really like to drive it around on the property. Although, it is quite difficult to get parts for it these days. Now ,how about we get in and go back to the house so we can have us some lunch?" Mrs. Robinson looked up as she climbed into the passenger side, smiling. Miles hesitated and looked over at her as if looking for some reassurance that it was safe to get into the truck and they were not going to take him back to that hell hole.

"What is wrong Miles?" Ma asked. "Well...I don't want to be any trouble and I really don't want to go back to my house. I am not sure this is a good idea after all" Miles said. "Well, what do you think is going to happen?" she said. "I don't know... I know that if I go back home, I will be in a lot of trouble" Miles said. Ma could see he was terrified and shaking. She could just see the fear in his eyes. "Miles, what will it take to convince you that we won't take you back there? I promise you we are not here to judge you or hurt you. We just want to help you and the only way we can do that is if you let us" Ma said.

Miles stood there for a short while and decided to take a chance. He had to trust someone at some point, and it would be better trust someone that he knew a little about who they were. "Can I ride in the back?" Miles asked. "You bet" Pa said. Miles climbed into the rear of the truck and moved to the front of the truck bed. Although he was very nervous and scared still, he was excited to be able to ride in this truck. He grabbed a hold of the rails and held on tight as Pa started to drive the truck forward.

As they drove along, Miles could see the apple orchard went on forever. They must have thousands of trees he thought. He looked along the road and he could see old apples had fallen from the trees.

He saw another truck with a load full of men going the opposite direction. They had ladders and baskets inside the bed of their truck. Miles thought they must be going to pick all of the ripe apples from the trees. As they arrived at the end of the orchard, he could see a large farm house with a porch that wrapped around the front of the house and there were a couple of barns.

Miles thought, boy these people must be rich! They had two huge barns with a big, long, tall round thing sticking up real high next to one of the barns. He didn't know what that was, but it was real big! Miles saw at least five horses and several cows along the way. Next to the house, there were pigs in a pen and several chickens running around in the yard.

The house was made of brick and wood. It was two stories and had a fireplace. Miles had only seen homes and barns like this once in movies and in some books that he had read. The porch covered the entire entrance of the house. The house's front steps had a brick wall on either side of them with big concrete posts located at the bottom of the steps. Sitting on top of each of these posts were cement statues of eagles.

Besides the house being huge, the wood on the top level was painted brown and the brick on the lower level was colored red. The left front of the house had a curved window, sticking out, and on the right side of the house was a really large window that went all of the way up to the second floor. Miles could see a stairway through this window. Once he jumped down from the truck bed, he walked up to the porch and saw a large, brown dog lying on a rug. The dog raised its head for a moment, just long enough to look up and see who was there. Then the dog laid its head back down and seemed to go back to sleep.

Mrs. Robinson smiles and said "That is Jake, he is our oldest member of the family. Been around for seventeen years." "Seventeen years, that's not much older than I am" Miles said. Mrs. Robinson started laughing and said "that would be seventeen dog years." "Oh, is that different?" Miles asked. "Oh heavens yes son, a dog ages seven years to every one year that we age" she responded. "Well, that doesn't sound fair. So that would make him one hundred and nineteen years old" he said. Mrs. Robinson smiled and said "well, I suppose you're right. That could be why he sleeps so much."

The kitchen was way over on the other side of the house from the front. They had to walk through three rooms to get there. Miles was amazed to see that each room was full of furniture. Big wooden cabinets full of dishes, couches, and chairs. Big chairs filled with cushions. One of the chairs had a handle on its side that let the chair lean back. Pictures hung up on the walls were as tall as Miles. There seemed to be a television in every room! In the next room over, the kitchen table, which could seat at least ten people, had a light hanging over it that looked like it had animal horns on it all the way around it. Each one of the horns had a light at the end of it.

Miles had never seen so much stuff in one place before. He was lucky to get one side of a bed to sleep in. His family only had one television and it didn't always work! Their dinner table only seated four people, so he had to sit on the floor to eat. Most of the cabinets were full of paper plates or dirty dishes. There was only one picture frame on the wall in that house and it had a tongue in it. Why he wasn't sure, but he had some guesses as to what that tongue meant and who had hung it up.

Making it into the kitchen, Mrs. Robinson pointed to a seat and told him to sit down. Walking over to the refrigerator, she asked if he wanted a glass of lemonade. Miles nodded his head. Pa walked in just after them and said "hey Ma, why don't you get me one of those too?" "Way ahead of you Pa" she said. As Ma was preparing their drinks, Pa sat down at the table and looked at Miles. "What is that big round thing next to your barn?" Miles asked. "It is a silo. We keep grain in it for the horses and cows we have. We also sell some of the grain to other local farmers" Pa said.

"What makes you ask that question?" Pa asked Miles ."I have never seen one before and did not know what it was. You must have a lot of grain in there. How do you get so much?" Miles asked. "We have a wheat farm on the back side of the property and we get the grain from there. Some of it we buy from farmers in other towns. We try to carry enough to supply the whole area" Pa said. As they were talking Jake, the dog, came into the room.

He walked over to Miles and placed his head on Miles's knee. At first Miles jumped and scared them both. Ma said "he wants you to pet him Miles. He won't hurt you." Miles reached out and put his right hand on Jakes head and started rubbing it side to side. Jake moved back and put his head back on Miles's knee. Miles sat there, rubbing Jake's head. He thought about how calming this felt. He had never been around animals much, other than the varmints at the trailer home park.

Now came the question Miles was dreading and hoping to avoid. "Miles, we really need to talk to you about why we found you in our apple tree field today. What happened at your home that caused you to feel the need to leave it?" Ma asked. Miles looked up and did not want to answer her. He was afraid if he did, one of two things are going to happen. First, they wouldn't believe him and second, they would call the police to come and take him back to his house. Either way, it did not end well for him. More likely, they would try to talk him into going back to his home.

Although, Miles had already considered trying to go back to his house, he had since decided against it. He was better off away from that hell hole! At this point, he had been gone long enough, that if he goes back, he just knew he would be beaten beyond recognition or locked inside that damn shed forever! If he went to the police, he figured they would either give him to with CPS, or put him in juvenile detention, or worse take him back to his house! In his mind, he thought he would just end up being punished severely and suffer the consequences of his actions. He was doomed whatever he said.

He would rather be let go and work this out for himself away from his house, or maybe they could just let him stay here for a while. "Mrs. Robinson, I am really thankful that both of you are trying to help me, but I am not sure you can. My thoughts are if I tell you what is really going on at my house, it could cause you and your family to be in a great deal of harm. Not to mention the harm that it would cause me!" Miles answered. "So what do you think we need to do?" Pa asked. "If you could let me stay here a few days, I can decide what I need to do next" Miles said in a low tone, hanging his head, afraid to look them in the eyes.

"As much as we would love to have you stay with us, our problem is more of a legal issue than anything. You are ten years old. We believe you have run away from your home and right now, we have no rights to make a decision about you ourselves. Our correct course of action would be to call the police and have them step in to help you. I sense from what you have said that idea would not out work well for you" Pa said. Miles looked up in total fear, as if he just threatened his life. "I am begging you! Please, please, please don't do that! Don't call the police!"

Ma looked back at Miles and said "then you are going to have to help us help you. We need some understanding of why you are sitting here in our kitchen. As a runaway, we are responsible for any decisions that we make about you at this point. I have been your teacher ever since you were in first grade, and I know you are a very bright and smart, young boy. You have to understand your situation from our point of view. We need to be able to follow certain laws to protect you and us. Do you understand?" "Yes" Miles said looking dejected and defeated.

"Then, how about we do this? We will ask you questions, and if you feel you can answer them, then you will answer them as best you can" Ma said. "We can try that" Miles said. Miles had his escape plans for a long time. He knew that in the end, he could not tell his full plans to anyone, even Ma and Pa. He couldn't tell them all of the truth. He had to play his cards close, so that he didn't look like he had this all planned out. He wanted them to believe him. He told himself that he must be careful and look really scared to convince them to let him stay, or at least, let him leave them.

"When did you run away?" Pa asked. "Yesterday afternoon. We were playing in the woods outside our trailer park" Miles said. "Who is we and where were you playing?" Pa asked. "Willy is my step-brother and he was with me. We had found some stuff that someone had thrown away down on the river bank. We were playing with it" Miles answered. "Is going to the woods and river something you do often?" Ma asked. "Sometimes, but my dad said not to the night before. He told us we would get bit by snakes or other varmints there" Miles said.

"So why did you go there after being told not to?" Pa asked. "I don't know. Willy talked me into it. We like, to go down there and explore. Sometimes, we find stuff…like once when I found this really cool rock" Miles said. "What kind of stuff did you find yesterday?" Ma asked. "A bicycle and Jumbo Jack Dump Truck, a big television, some tires, and a computer. There was other stuff there, but we didn't geta chance to keep looking through it" Miles answered. "Why not?" Pa asked. "Because Jimmy started hollering our names. He was looking for us" Miles said.

"Who is Jimmy?" Ma asked. "Jimmy is one of my older brothers" Miles said. "How many siblings do you have?" Ma asked. "What are siblings?" he asked. "Brothers and sisters" Ma said. "Do stepbrothers and a sister count?" Miles asked. "Yes" she said. "Lewis is my oldest brother, then Jimmy is next, then Carolyn is my younger sister. Rebecca is my oldest stepsister, and Willy is my step-brother" Miles explained.

"So what happened after Jimmy showed up and started calling your names?" Pa asked. "Well…we put all of the stuff back and hid it under some bushes so maybe no one else would find them. Then Willy and I ran up the hill.

Willy ran back to the left and I went to the right. We did not want them to know where we had been, so we were planning to come up at different areas. I came up to the top and Willy stayed down" Miles said. "Jimmy can be a pain in the ass because he was always trying to get us into trouble with my stepmom! He tattles on us all the time!" Miles continued.

"So what happened when you came up to the top?" Pa pushed a little. "My stepmom was with Jimmy and she had her whip in her hand" Miles said. "I'm sorry…her what?" Ma said. "Her Whip. It has a leather wrap about three feet long on it. And at one end, it has a handle with a metal bar inside of it. On the other end, it has strands of leather with nails on them" Miles said. "What does she use that for?" Pa asked. Miles looked up and this is where he decided he has had enough. This train was coming to a stop and he could not ride any longer. "Look, I told you I am not sure I can do this!" Miles said. "We understand" Pa said.

"You do?" Miles said. "Of course we do" Pa said. "No one in this house wants you to feel as if any story you tell us will embarrass you or cause you any harm. We need you to feel okay with talking to us. If we have to wait a little while, then we will" he finished. "Well, thank you. I guess I will give you an answer" feeling like he was back on the train Miles thought. "She makes us strip down. Then Jimmy ties us to a tree located right outside the woods at the end for the trailer park. Then she beats us with her whip until we pass out. They come back later and cut us down. Then she locks us inside the shed beside the house!" Miles explained, tears gathering in his eyes.

"The shed has a chain that is welded to a rod that is cemented to the floor and at the end of the chain is a shackle. She ties that shackle onto our legs and locks us inside. We stay in there until my Dad gets home or she decides it is time to let us out. Then she would tell my Dad how we defied his orders. If he is sober enough, he takes us out back and beats us again with his belt!" he continued.

By this time, Miles had tears running down his face. He had trouble finishing the story because he is shaking and crying now, trying to hold it together. The whole time he was looking at the floor with his head down and not even looking up throughout his whole story.

It was really quiet in the house at this point. Both Ma and Pa were just sitting there, staring at each other. Miles finally looked up to see the look on their faces. He asked "is there anything else you want to know?" "Is this when you ran away?" Ma asked. "No. When Willy hid and did not come to the top, my stepmom sent Jimmy after him. The last thing I saw was Jimmy pulling Willy up the hill dragging him by his foot, kicking and screaming! The next thing I knew, I looked at my step-mom and said fuck this and I ran! I couldn't let them do this to me anymore!" Miles paused as he finished his story.

"I am sorry for cussing but that is what happened" Miles said. "I think that will be okay this time" Pa said. "I wanted to go back and get Willy, but I couldn't last night! I was just so scared, and hungry and tired from running. I am sorry about your apples. I will pay you back. Please don't make me go back there! Please! I swear I will be good and you won't even know I am here! I can sleep in the barn or in the woods. Just don't make me go back there!" Miles began begging. "Now, slow down son. We are not going to send you back there. I really don't want you living off my apple trees either!" Pa said. Ma turned around and walked out of the room. Miles couldn't see her face because she was trying to hide her tears.

So now Miles has released the Kraken. The monster he has never spoke of. Now he waits to see how this is going to play out. Will all of his fears become a reality? "Look, we need to determine if what you are saying is true. Because if I go to the police and present this story to them, they are going to want to check it out. These are some pretty serious accusations here that could cause your family major harm. Also, we are not here to throw you back into an environment that is harmful to you. Before we make any decisions, we need to verify what you are saying is true" Pa said. At this time Ma returned to the room to continue our conversation.

"No!" Miles said. "We cannot go to the police! They will make me go back to that hell hole or they will turn me over to CPS! Then I will end up in some home of someone I don't know! Or they will send me to juvenile detention! I want to stay here. I know Mrs. Robinson from school and she is nice to me. I don't want to go anywhere else!" Pa said "CPS...where is this coming from? Jesus son slow down! None of these things are going to happen until Ma and I look into this." "I told you he was smart. It's a shame he probably knows more about the system than we do. He shouldn't even know what CPS is" Ma said. "Miles, what does CPS stand for?" frustrated as she turns and asked him.

"Child Protective Services" he answered. "What do you think they do?" she asked. "They take kids from their homes and put them in foster homes" Miles said. "No, they don't. When a family has a complaint against them, CPS investigates the complaint. If they find an issue, they can and will remove the children from the home, but only if there is an issue. Children are not just tossed into foster care because they want to get rid of them. Children that are placed in foster homes are put there because they have no family to go home to. Most children in broken homes end up with other family members.

"So I wouldn't end up in foster care?" Miles asked. "If what you are saying is true about what is happening in your home, then we will do whatever we can to help you find a good home to live in; along with your brothers and sisters. So, how do we figure out if what you are telling us is true?" Pa looked at Miles and asked. As Pa asked this question, Ma looked over at him and said "can we step into the other room and talk and let him think about this?" she asked Pa.

Pa said "give me a moment to talk to Ma, okay?" "Okay" Miles said. "Would you like something to eat? Maybe some chips?" "No thank you" Miles answered. Pa leaves the room with Ma to talk. She moved into the dining room so that she could express her feelings without Miles hearing her. As Ma sat down in one of the chairs, she started crying. Pa also sat down at the table with her and tried to console her. Miles can barely hear them from where he is located, but he can hear what they are saying. Ma said "how could I have missed this? There had to be signs, right? I never saw them!" "You sure he is telling the truth?" Pa asked. "Oh yes, I know for that sure! He is not the type of boy to make up a story like that! I just cannot understand how I did not see this! I knew he was having some issues...but not to this level!" Ma is questioning her own judgement of Miles, wondering how she could not have seen any of this trauma.

Miles stood up from the table and walked over to the room where they were at. He stood just outside the door and listened to what they were saying. He didn't understand why she was questioning herself, when she had done nothing wrong. When she stopped talking and was able to wipe her eyes, Miles stuck his head around the corner and said "it's not your fault. We have been told all our lives that if we tell any part of what is happening at home, it will lead to us getting into even more trouble! I have seen what my stepmother does and until now, I have not had the courage to run away or tell anyone what was happening" Miles said!

"Well, I am so sorry I never saw that you were being hurt and traumatized at home" Ma said. Pa looked over at Miles and said "you realize how serious all of this is?" "Yes sir, I do" Miles responded. "I have never told anyone about this before now. I have always just tried to stay out of trouble and not give my stepmother any reason to want to punish us. Lately, she has been on the war path! I don't know why.

For some reason, she has been having Jimmy watch us even more than usual and we get in trouble for nothing!" Miles continued. "Willy and I decided a long time ago we were going to try and run away. We were supposed to leave together, but I had to leave him behind yesterday. Now, I don't know what they have done to him! I don't know how I am going to be able to get him out of there!" Miles finished.

As he stood there, both Ma and Pa were staring at him, then Pa said "well, if what you are saying is true, we will need to prove it." Miles stepped into the room with his head hanging down and tears welling up in his eyes as he turned around and raised his shirt up then pulled his pants down slightly to show all the scars from the whippings. His whole lower back and bottom was riddled with huge scars, some up to six inches long! One scar went from his right shoulder all the way down to his bottom! It was as if the whip got stuck and she ripped it out of him! Scars on top of scars, evidence of numerous beatings! Some of his scars still had scabs on them. Ma placed her hand over her mouth and whispered "oh my God!" She began crying uncontrollably. She stood up and reached out to give Miles a hug. He pulled back, as if to say wait...there's more. He bent over and pulled both pants legs up to his knees. That's when they could see the scarring on his ankles. Recent red marks and scabs from the shackles were still visible. "Oh my

God!" Ma said looking back at Pa, who now also had tears forming in his eyes.

Miles stood there exposed and scared that showing the evidence that he was being truthful would only make things worse for him. "So now what?" Miles asked. "What happens now? I know you are not my family. I am sorry for getting you involved in my mess. I just don't know what else to do! Maybe, if my Dad would just let us go back to my Grandpa and Grandma's house, we would be okay." "Well, first off don't apologize. No child should have to worry about or deal with this kind of stuff. I don't know the answer yet to that question Miles. I honestly have never had to deal with anything like this. So I am going to have to find someone I can ask. The only people I know are some friends of ours who are on the police force. I can safely call them" Pa said.

"Oh man! I knew this was going to happen! I will be back at that house before the sun goes down!" Miles said. "Like hell you will! You will never have to go back to that house if I have anything to say about it! Pa, get on the phone and call Bruce and get him out here. I promise you this is not going to turn out the way you think it is Miles. I will see to that!" Ma shouted. As Pa made the call, Ma reached out to Miles and gave him a big hug telling him "I am so sorry for not noticing something was wrong. I am so sorry." Miles was in shock. Nobody had ever stood up for him like this nor shown any kind of compassion for his situation. Of course, he has never told anyone about the abuse before that is happening at that house.

Pa called Bruce on the phone and said "hey Bruce, I need you to come out to the house today. Yeah, we have a situation out here and we need your help and advice with it." After waiting just a short while, Police Officer Bruce arrived at the house.

Pa greeted him at the front door and said "we have a nasty situation here. We found a young boy in our apple orchard this morning, and after some time and conversation, we have found his home situation is not at all safe. In fact, it is downright abusive! I think that after you hear what this boy has to say and what he has showed us, you will understand why. I would like to see what we need to do to allow him to stay here while you verify his story."

"Okay" Officer Bruce responded. "You seem pretty concerned. Do you know who he is and where he lives?" "Yes. His name is Miles Dingwald, but I am not certain where he lives. It is possible Ma may have that piece of information, because he is one of her students. I would prefer we let him explain the rest" said Pa. "Well...that explains the concern I guess, it's personal. Why call me? Why not call his parents?" asked Officer Bruce. "Again, I would ask that we let him tell you his story. Once you see and hear what he has shared with us, hopefully you can help us" said Pa.

They walked into the house and Pa introduced Miles to Officer Bruce. "Miles, this is Officer Bruce from our local Police Department. He is a friend of mine and Ma's. He has been around our family for a long time, so we trust him to be able to help us. I believe you can trust him too. Are you willing to try that?" "I will try" Miles said.

As Miles looked up at Officer Bruce and panicked! His eyes grew wider and his face turned red. His heart began to race and fear set in as he recognized this officer from a visit to his home the week before. "I know you" Officer Bruce said. "You're one of the Dingwald children. You live over there at the trailer park on old Robinson Road. You have a brother, Willy, right?" Miles drops his head and said "he is my step-brother." Officer Bruce turned and looked at Pa and said "we had a call from a neighbor about his step-brother last week. The neighbor said they were locking the step-brother, Willy, up in the shed outside the house and leaving him there for days. We responded and took a look around, but did not find any evidence at that time. Willy was not in the shed at the time of our visit. Their Mom said he was out in the woods playing. I remember you Miles was standing right outside the house with two other siblings.

"Your Mom said the neighbor needs to mind their own business. She said they use that shed to lock their goat up at night. They have a spike and chain welded inside to hold the goat. When I asked where the goat was she said 'in the field, over past the trees, grazing. I send the boys over there, before dark, to round it up.' We looked around but didn't see any signs of the boy and no signs of a goat. All the other children looked pretty healthy, so we just kicked it off as an angry neighbor. It was the neighbor's word against your Mom's and there wasn't any evidence or signs of abuse so we left. So where was Willy that night?" he asked Miles. "He couldn't walk very well, so he was asleep in the bedroom" Miles said.

"So, what brings you to the Robinson house today?" Officer Bruce asked. Pa looked up at Miles and said "okay Miles, I want you to tell Officer Bruce what you told us. Show him your back and ankles." Miles looked up, fearing this was only going to end up the way he predicted. He was hesitant in saying anything to anyone in the first place. He looked down at the ground and thought, if he doesn't say anything, then the officer will go away and leave him here. Just as the thought passed through his head, Ma turned and said "Miles, if you don't talk, then all of this will be for nothing. Officer Bruce will be forced to take you back to that house and we don't want that for you."

"We brought Officer Bruce here because we know he will listen to you and try to help. I promise you can trust him and tell him the truth. Would you like him to ask you questions like we did?" she asked Miles. He shook his head no; he knew it was now or never. He has to tell someone the truth; otherwise his life will be over. Miles turned towards Officer Bruce, with tears in his eyes and fear in his heart and began telling him the story he told Ma and Pa.

"Yesterday, Willy and I were playing in the woods even though my Dad had told us not too. We had found a bunch of stuff that was thrown into the river. It looked like new stuff. We were investigating it, at least until we heard Jimmy calling us. My brother, Jimmy, told my step-mom that we had gone down there and they had come looking for us. We tried to hide the stuff we found and then we split up. I went one direction and Willy ran the other way. Our plan was to come out away from where we were separately so they wouldn't know about the stuff we found. As I came out the top, they saw me but Willy saw that my step-mom was there and carrying her whip. So he stopped and did not come out the top. They did not see him. We both knew that anytime she had that stupid whip it was a bad thing!" Miles said.

"Mom sent Jimmy to fetch Willy. And when he found him, he dragged him by his feet up the hill as he was heading to the tree" Miles explained. "The tree?" said Officer Bruce questioning. "Yes, there is a tree inside the trailer park ,just at the edge of the woods that she makes us strip down and ties us to it. She then takes her whip and whips us until we can't stand up anymore!" Miles continues. Officer Bruce looked over at Ma and Pa, looking a little confused. He stared at Miles a minute, then asked him "what kind of stuff did you find? You said it looked new. What was down there?"

Pa looked over at Officer Bruce like "really...that's your take on all of this!" he thought. Bruce looked over at Pa and waved him off, as if to tell him to just be patient. Bruce knew that there had been recent burglaries in the surrounding neighborhoods. He wanted to see if this was the same stuff. Miles looked up at him confused and began to tell him what they had found. Miles told him about the bike, the dump truck, TV, laptop, tires, and a whole host of other things they saw but never got the chance to really look at.

"Well" Bruce said "I believe you have something you wanted to show me as well." Miles turned and looked at Pa and Ma. This will be the second time in his life he has ever showed anyone the truth. Even in gym at school, he didn't pull off his shirt. Miles was very hesitant; his heart is racing so fast he felt as if it was going to jump out of his chest. "Go ahead" Pa said gently. "Give him a little bit. Can't you see he is scared to death?" Ma said. "Miles, I know you don't know me or trust me. You see this badge I am wearing. It requires me to uphold the law and follow an ethical code. I really like my job and I believe that when someone is hurting children, it makes me very upset. However, in order for me to help you, I need to know what is going on and what they are doing to you" Officer Bruce tried to reassure Miles.

"What does an ethical code mean?" Miles asked. "It means that I have certain rules I have to follow to protect and serve the community. I have to make sure that my officers and I do everything we can to provide you and everyone around you with a safe environment" Officer Bruce said. Miles looked up at Officer Bruce with tears in his eyes and even though he was still scared, he felt a little more comfortable. He then turned around began to pull up his shirt, so that the officer could see the scars. Then he pulled up his pants leg to show him the scars from the shackles on his ankles.

Miles turned and looked at Officer Bruce and said "by the way, Officer Bruce, what is the slang name for goat?" Officer Bruce looks at him with a look of confusion and mumbles 'kid', oh...kid he thinks, goat! "Oh my God! It was a play on words! Wow! I never would have gotten that one" Officer Bruce admits. "Thank you Miles for trusting me enough to show me your evidence and allow me to move forward with an investigation. Would you mind if Ma, Pa, and I step out of the room so we could talk?" Officer Bruce asked. "Okay" said Miles. Ma looked over and said "if you want something to snack on, just go ahead into the kitchen and there are some snacks on the table."

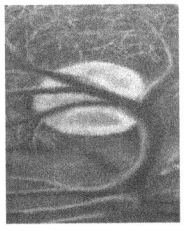

CHAPTER 3- THE STORY BEGINS

Officer Bruce, Pa, and Ma walked out of the room, only this time Pa took him to the back of the house, so that Miles could not hear them talk. If only that were true. Again, Miles sneaks quietly after them, next to the room that they were in where they could not see him. Officer Bruce turned and began talking to Pa and Ma. "Early this morning, we had a call come in about a small boy found on the side of the road, over past the Old Robinson area."

"He was about a mile or two down the road. When we arrived, it looked like he had been run over by a car. We were not able to identify him at that time, but he was still alive. That child is in a coma at the hospital now. It looked like a car tried to run him over more than once! He appeared to be about Mile's age. Now that I heard Miles's story, he may be the stepbrother Willy that Miles was referring to. I am going to call in our forensic group and have them come over here, so we can get some evidence and pictures of Miles's back and ankles. And also check him for any other injuries. I will speak to the Child Protective Services (CPS) manager and see if he can stay here until we can get more results from our investigation. Also just to clarify for you, the reason I wanted to know what stuff they had found was because we have had a rash of local thefts, just north of that trailer park. I wanted to see if the stuff he found was some of it. Are you okay with that?"

Miles stepped out from behind the wall in the room next door. "Damn it boy! Can't you follow a simple instruction? If we wanted you to hear what we said, we would have brought you with us!" Pa said. Miles dropped his head as he didn't want Pa to be angry with him. Although he looked back up and with an angry stare said "he is my brother and I want to know what has happened to him! If it is him, I can help you identify him. You better hope it's not him because if they hurt my brother, I will go back to that house and do the job you should have done a week ago!"

"Hold on now Miles" Pa said. "Let's just settle down and let Officer Bruce do his job. I understand you may think you can go beat everybody up. If you could have, you already would have done so I imagine. After everything you have been through, we want to make sure we follow the letter of the law to help keep this from happening again. Secondly, Officer Bruce is going to bring in a group of investigators to gather evidence from you that can provide evidence of your abuse." "Well...I am not impressed with the job the police have done so far!" Miles said. "Officer Bruce was standing right in front of that shed and he didn't do anything last week!"

Ma said "Miles come over here. You need to calm down and let us help you. We need to do this the right way. Hurting them or doing more bad things will not fix this. Officer Bruce, would it help if he came to the hospital and looked at the boy there?" "Actually, it would. It's late today, so why don't we set it up and meet there in the morning? I will call the CPS Manager here in a little while and see if I can get an answer as to whether or not Miles can stay here for now." Miles turned and looked at the officer and said "you make sure you do your job this time! There is plenty of evidence at that house to see what they are doing!" Miles stormed away and went back into the kitchen. Ma followed him.

"You're being a little hard on him, don't you think Miles? He is only doing his job" Ma said. "Well...I am sorry I guess. I don't mean to be hard on him or mean. I just wished he would have paid more attention that day he came out last week! Maybe Willy would not be in the hospital now if he had!" Miles exclaimed. Officer Bruce spent the next hour calling his station, gathering up some officers and one or two forensic personnel to get the investigation started. He knew he was going to have to spend a lot of time working with the other officers, providing them with information. This would be his first major abuse case and he wanted to make sure they followed the investigation by the book.

He called the CPS manager and said "Mrs. Johnson, this is Officer Bruce from the Little Elm Police Department. I need to talk to you about a case we have that is being filed tonight concerning child abuse and possible attempted murder. One of the children involved has ran away from that home and has ended up over at Mayor Robinson's home. This young boy is one of Mrs. Robinson's students. Due to the nature of the case, they are requesting that we allow the child to stay at their home until we determine the outcome of this case. Is this possible and what do they need to do to make that happen?" "Well...all they need is to do is be granted temporary guardianship of him and then they can keep him there as long as needed. Is that what you want to do?" she asked.

"Yes. Can he stay there tonight? Also, we may have another child as well from the same family involved in this case. We are going to the hospital in the morning to identify that poor boy" Officer Bruce explained. "Yes, the boy at Mayor Robinson's house can stay with them overnight. I will treat it as if we did not get this case's notification until tomorrow morning. I will have to get the documents together and take them to the Judge tomorrow. It's late now, so we can do this first thing in the morning. Text me the boy's information and I will do some of the paperwork tonight. Mayor Robinson and his wife will have to come down to the courthouse to sign some forms tomorrow" she explained.

As the officers arrived with two forensic personnel, they began to approach Miles to get any evidence needed to support and start the investigation. Miles backed away from these strangers and moved closer to Ma. Although he knew this was coming, it frightened him about what would happen if he told anyone and this was never a part of his plans. He always thought he could just tell his story, show his back, and then that would be it. Now, he was going to be poked and prodded and he was not sure this was something he could do. The lead forensic technician approached him very slowly and began to talk. "Miles, my name is Officer Glen and I work for the police department. My job is to gather as much evidence as I can on your injuries, so that we can test them for DNA and particulates that may offer us more knowledge that we can use to make sure the people that caused your injuries pay for hurting you. Do you understand?"

"What are particulates?" Miles asked. "Well…they are tiny, little particles of stuff that might get imbedded in wounds and on other areas. If we can identify them, we can try to match it to the weapon that was used to hurt you." "Weapon? It was a whip with small nails in the tip! Not a weapon!" Miles responded. "If the whip was used and caused you harm, then it is considered a weapon" the officer said. 'Oh' thought Miles. He had never heard of that before. "Would you mind if Rose and I see your injuries and perform some tests on them? It would really help us with our investigation." Officer Glen stated. "Will it hurt?" Miles asked. "Not at all" he replied. "Okay" Miles said as he turned and raised his shirt. "Oh my god" the female tech said out loud. The forensic team began to take pictures from every angle and retrieve particles from of his injuries.

For the rest of the evening, the forensic team gathered as much information and evidence from Miles as they could, over and over; to the point that his eyes started to close with exhaustion. Seeing this, Officer Bruce said "okay that's enough for today. I will see you in the morning son. Oh and I spoke with Jan Johnson, our CPS manager, and she has granted Ma and Pa the okay let you stay with them overnight. However tomorrow morning, she will take a document to the Judge to get Ma and Pa temporary guardianship of you. It will have to be signed by both of Ma and Pa before it is presented to the Judge. This document, once approved by the judge, will allow you to stay here with Ma and Pa while the investigation is occurring." Officer Bruce walked through the house and found Pa. He provided Pa with the same information including telling him that, "I also let Ms. Johnson know that we may have to do this again for the other boy. I hope that was okay with you Pa?" Officer Bruce. "Yes, that is fine. We will see you in the morning when you come by for breakfast with us" Pa said.

Mrs. Robinson looked over at Miles and asked "are you hungry? I can make us some dinner if you like. Do you have a favorite food?" Miles looked up at her and said "yes ma'am I am hungry. I am not picky, just whatever you want to make is fine." "Okay" she said. "Pa, what do you want for supper?" "Oh man, let me think on it" Pa said. "Um, maybe some of those little pizza things you make?"

Ma smiled, she knew that he was talking about pizza rolls. Easy to make and she liked easy. Ma gathered the pizza roll bag out of the freezer and put them in a pan. She set the oven's temperature and placed the pan into the oven. Then she set her timer. Afterwards she made a pitcher of sweet tea. Then she sat down with Miles to wait for the pizza rolls to cook. "Am I going to be okay?" Miles asked. "Yes, Miles you will be. Right now we don't know how all of this is going to play out. Where you will end up or who you will be living with after the investigation" Ma said. Miles looked at her and said "it's real nice here" and smiled at her. She smiled back.

"What kind of drink is this I have? It's really good. I have never had any drink like this before" Miles said. Ma smiled and looked up and said "sweet tea, my specialty." "Well, it sure is good" he said as he gulped down another big swallow. Ding, ding, ding, the timer went off. Ma reached over to get a pot holder to pull the pizza rolls out of the oven. She placed them on the stove and called Pa to come in for dinner. He had finished up with the police and Officer Bruce was the last to leave. By the time he got into the house, Miles was already finished with his first serving of pizza rolls. Pa looked back after getting his plate and asked "want some more?" Miles nodded his head and stood up to take his plate over.

Pa put more of the pizza rolls on it. "Have you tried this sauce on yours? Ma makes it home made. It's real good" Pa said. "No sir, but I would like to try some if it's okay" Miles responded. After all he has been through today, Miles was pretty beat. "Am I going to sleep here tonight Mrs. Robinson?" Miles asked.

"Well, I believe after the day we have had, you can call me Ma. But to answer your question, yes. Pa can you help me get the back room put together with the bed you will sleep in. You can sleep there tonight and I will clean up the old guest room for you to use after tonight." "Okay" Pa said. After that Miles thought this sounds promising. Maybe his wish to stay with Ma and Pa will come true.

"You like those pizza rolls Miles?" Ma asked. "Oh yes ma'am, they were great! But this tea is awesome too!" Miles said. Pa laughed and said "yes she makes the best sweet tea." "Well, let's get your room set up so we can all get some sleep. Tomorrow will be a long day and we have a lot of chores to get done before we can leave to go downtown" Pa said.

Both Ma and Pa led the way down the back hallway to a small room at the end of the hall. Ma stopped on the way at a closet and reached inside to remove a set of sheets and pillow cases for his bed. As Pa entered the room, he had to move some boxes stored in a corner. Together they placed the sheets on the bed and put pillow cases on two pillows. Once the room was ready, Pa took off and left Ma to finish up. Ma gave Miles some of her grandson's sleeping clothes. They fit just fine but Miles was not a Marvel comic character fan. Oh well he thought, it's better than sleeping in my dirty clothes.

Ma took his old clothes and said she would put them in the washer and clean them. She handed Miles a new pair of pants and shirt to wear tomorrow. "See if these fit you" she said. "We don't have an extra pair of tennis shoes though that I think would fit you." "What are tennis shoes?" Miles asked. "She looked over at Miles confused and pointed to his shoes he was wearing. "You mean sneakers" Miles said. "Okay sneakers. I don't have an extra pair of sneakers for you" she said as she smiled. "Get some rest and I will see you in the morning. Good night Miles." "Ma, thank you and tell Pa I said thank you too" Miles said. She stopped, turned around, and smiled back at him, then turned and headed out of the room.

This room was twice the size of any room Miles had ever slept in before. The bed was huge and soft and no springs were sticking out of its mattress. The covers actually went past the bed sides. The walls had pictures of all sorts of people on them. Miles assumed these were family pictures. A window on one of the walls had a view of the barn across the yard. Miles could see out of the window from the bed. Even with all the lights turned off, he could still see in his room because the moon was shining in. He liked that it was like having a natural night light and wasn't so dark.

The furniture in the room was framed with rustic wood. The wood itself was made from tree limbs that someone had put together. Miles looked at the bed and was really amazed at how someone would know how to cut a hole in the end of the bed and slip the end of a tree limb into it. As he looked underneath the bottom of his bed, it had these cuts that were half way through the boards that overlapped back and forth. This was so cool! I wonder if I could learn to make furniture like this, 'he thought'.

Miles lay down on the bed and began thinking about the events of the day. He realized that he could never return to his home now. Whether he would ever get to see Willy or any of his brothers and sisters again, he didn't know. This had been such an exhausting day. Never in a million years did he believe he could have the strength to leave that house or tell anyone about his life there. He was so tired, that he didn't even think about going into his dream world that he usually needed to go to sleep.

Instead, he must have fallen a sleep because the next thing he saw was sunlight shining through his window. It was quite bright and no matter which way he turned, all he saw was sun. The window had drapes unlike what they used at home, which was normally just an old, dirty sheet. Miles tried to close them, but could not figure out how to do so.

He decided it was time to get up. Today, he was going to go to the hospital to see if the other boy was Willy that Officer Bruce had mentioned. He was pretty sure it was. After he used the bathroom and took a shower, he started getting ready and noticed that the clothes Ma had given him had a pair of boots located underneath them. Miles had never had a pair of boots before. He put on the jeans, shirt, socks, and boots. He was not sure about the boots, but the clothes were really nice he thought. Off to the kitchen he went hoping he could find it. He wasn't paying attention last night on how they got to his room because he could barely keep his eyes open at that time.

As he walked down the hallway, he looked at the pictures of the children hanging up on the hallway's walls. There were a lot of them. It looked like the same two kids, over and over, only they appeared to be older in some of the pictures. As he got closer to the kitchen, he heard Pa talking to someone. He turned the last corner and smelled something that he liked. As he entered the kitchen, Officer Bruce looked up and said "well, good morning Miles. I hope you had pleasant night." "It was really nice. I never had a bed to myself before. It was really big and so soft and the bed was really cool! It was made from tree limbs! Have you talked to the hospital yet about the boy there? How is the little boy doing that we are going to see?" Miles asked.

"Well, I have spoken to the hospital and he still has not woken up yet. But he is breathing. He seems to be having quite a bit of a struggle. The doctors say it was truly a miracle that he was still alive! We believe he was out there lying in the ditch for most of the night before we found him" answered Officer Bruce. "What time will we be leaving here to go see him?" Miles asked. Pa looked up and said "we need to eat breakfast first, then you and I are going to feed the pigs and chickens. By then the hospital will be able to let us go in and see him. At some point today, we need to go by the courthouse and sign a waiver for guardianship form concerning you that allows you to stay with us." "Okay. But I don't know nothing about feeding chickens or pigs" said Miles. "Anything" Ma corrected Miles. Miles looked up confused. Ma said "I don't know anything about feeding chickens or pigs." "Oh...anything" he repeated back.

"What does guardianship mean? What's for breakfast? I am really hungry." Miles said. "Same as always...eggs, bacon, and biscuits" Pa said. "Everyday?"

Miles looks up surprised. He sat down at the table and watched as Office Bruce finished up his breakfast. Office Bruce looked up at Pa and said "I will see you up at the hospital when you are done. We can go over the rest of this then." "Okay" said Pa. Miles wanted to ask them what they were talking about but chose not to. He would wait to ask about what they were talking about after Officer Bruce had left. "Guardianship is a legal process that allows us to take care of you and act in your best interest. It will let you stay here until we can get a better idea of what comes next" Pa said.

Ma placed a plate in front of Miles and he looked down at it and paused. That's a lot of food for breakfast he thought. Officer Bruce left and Miles waited for a right moment to ask what was going on. Pa walked Officer Bruce out the door. As Pa reentered the room, he looked over at Miles and said "we have more information about the young boy at the hospital. It appears his injuries are pretty severe. The doctors have determined the reason he is having such a hard time breathing is that the whole right side of his ribs are broken or cracked. His right upper shoulder where the ball and joint are located, are also broken off, as well as his hip is broken off. The humorous or upper bone in his right arm is also broken."

"Officer Bruce wanted to let us know so we wouldn't be shocked when we saw him at the hospital. Your job is to identify him if you can. We don't want to bring your parents in just yet until we determine if this Willy or not. Once we know that answer, and if it does turns out to be him, Officer Bruce is going to gather a group officers, along with CPS and forensics, and go over to your house. Then the investigation can continue there. He is going to call the Judge this morning and get a warrant to search your home and property. Once we can confirm whether or not this is Willy, they will add that to the investigation information.

"Can we go with him?" Miles asked. "Why?" asked Pa. "So I can see their faces when they arrest them" said Miles. "I don't think that will be necessary. I think we need to let the law do what they are paid to do. However, we can holster that idea until after we are done at the hospital. If Officer Bruce sees any value in your presence there, then we will decide then. Fair enough?" Pa said. "Fair enough" Miles responded. Then he grinned and said under his breath 'holster that idea' who speaks like that. Pa just smiled and then turned as he walked out. "Let's go. We have to feed the chickens and pigs before we leave."

Miles had never been around farm animals before. Raccoons and armadillos were about all he had seen. I don't think those are farm animals though he thought. Although, he always thought of them as varmints. At their house, they would chase them and see who could kill the most. At the barn, Pa filled two large bean cans full of seed and handed one to Miles. Then he grabbed a big bag with a pig on it that was another type of feed. He lifted this large pig bag over his shoulder and said "come on follow me." Miles followed him over to the pig pen. Pa took the pig bag of feed and using his bright red Swiss army knife, he cut open the top of the bag.

He looked over at Miles and said, "whatever you do, don't get in that pen with those pigs or they will have you for breakfast! They are real hungry right now and they are not picky to what they eat!" "Then how are we going to feed them?" Miles asked. Pa lifted the bag back over his shoulder and leaned over the side of the fence, tilting the bag over what looked like a trough. "Just like this" Pa said. As the feed from the bag flowed out into the trough, the pigs came running and grunting over to the trough and immediately began eating. Biting each other and pushing to get at the feed. There were about ten pigs and they were definitely hungry.

"Wow! Looks like my house at dinner time!" Miles exclaimed. Pa laughed, although in the back of his mind, he wondered how much truth there was to what Miles told him. "Now the chickens" Pa said. "Do I need to worry about them trying to eat me too?" asked Miles. Pa smiled back and said "well...I wouldn't stick my hand out where they can reach it. But if you move quickly and just toss the feed out, they won't bother you." With the chickens, Miles stuck his hand in their feed bucket and started flinging the seed out of it onto the ground in their pen, watching as the chickens took off after the dropped seed and started eating.

There were probably thirty or so chickens, so he spread out the seeds throughout their pen. He looked up and saw that Pa was standing there watching him.

"Okay…am I doing this wrong or what? Why are you staring at me?" he asked. "No. But I was done a long time ago. I'm just waiting for you to get done." "Well, I am done now. Are we going to the hospital now?" he asked.

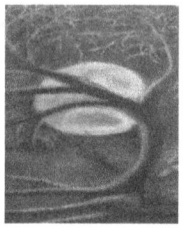

CHAPTER 4- IS IT WILLY

"Let's go get Ma and load up into the car. Then we can get going" Pa responded. "Why are we not taking the Model TT?" Miles asked. "That's a farm truck" said Ma. "We take something a little more civilized when we go into town" as they loaded up into a brand new Cadillac Seville. It had leather seats and smelled so sweet Miles thought. He looked into the front seat and saw on the dash what he thought was a small TV. "You have a TV in your car?" Miles said surprised.

Ma laughed and said "that's not a TV! It's a GPS system. It helps us get where we are going hopefully." Pa sat down in the driver's seat and started the car. He looked up in the rearview mirror and put on his seat belt. Then Pa turned back and told Miles to put his seat belt on. "My what? Seat belt? What is that?" Miles asked. Pa looked at Ma and took a deep breath as he opened his door and got out of the car, leaving the car running. Pa opened the back door and reached in and pulled Miles over to the left side of the car. Then he pulled out Miles' seat belt and said "seat belt." He reached around Miles and clicked it into place over Miles' chest and lap. "Oh. We don't have these in our car" Miles said. Pa got back in at the driver's seat, put on his own seat belt back on, put the car into drive, and off they went.

It took a while to get into town. Miles did not realize the town they lived in had so many houses, buildings and really big stores. He was fascinated and said to Ma "what are those places?" She looked back and said "well Miles, that's the mall. Have you never been there?" "No ma'am. I have never been to this part of town. I didn't know it was this big" Miles replied. Pa said "did you think it was just a trailer park and a school?" Ma slapped Pa's arm and said "Pa, be nice." He just laughed.

"Well I guess I never thought about it to be honest" Miles said. "Well, maybe we can take you to the mall sometime Miles. I don't know if today will work out that way, but maybe later on" Ma said. "I would appreciate that" Miles responded. Pa slowed down and took a right turn towards a really tall building. Miles looked up and saw what appeared to be a courthouse building. Pa found a parking spot and pulled into it and parked. Pa said to Miles "we need to go in here and see the Judge. I expect you to be on your best behavior." "Yes sir" Miles said.

As they entered the building, there were these large metal gates that were right inside the door. They had to stop and go through the metal gates one at a time. Both Ma and Pa had to put their personal belongings in their pockets and Ma's purse inside a box onto a moving rubber or plastic belt that moved over a table before they could walk through the gate. Their stuff disappeared into a tunnel-like box and a person outside this box was watching the people, moving belt, and what looked like a TV screen.

Once they walked through the gate and gathered their belongings off the belt on the other side of the box, Pa started walking towards an elevator. This place was really cool Miles thought. The building was really tall and the carvings on the ceiling looked like little people. The walls had tall pillars on them that went from the ground on up to the ceiling. All the windows were stained glass and had pictures in them.

Miles had never been in an elevator or seen such a building before in his life. As they stepped into the elevator he stood in the middle. When Pa pushed a button and the door closed, Miles moved to the side and grabbed a bar on a wall. It sounded like a motor started and the elevator seemed to move with a jerk. It made Miles head swirl and he felt light headed. He wasn't sure which way the elevator was moving, but he guessed up because some numbers were being lit up on a wall by the door were increasing. Up and up the elevator seemed to go, until the number six was lit up and the elevator's door opened.

When they stepped out of the door, Pa turned to the right and started walking down a big hallway. This hallway was not as big as the lower floor's hallway. As they reached a door, Pa turned and told Miles to sit down on a bench located outside of the doorway. Miles did as he told him. Pa knocked on the door, a girl opened the door, and let Pa and Ma inside, closing the door. Miles sat there looking around, trying to be quiet and good as Pa had instructed him to do.

As he began to look around, he noticed that there was not very many people there. So Miles started getting really bored. He felt like he was there forever. He hated not hearing what they were saying inside the room they went into. Then Pa and Ma came out. Ma had a folder in her hand with a bunch of papers in it. "Well that was interesting" Pa said. "A lot more paperwork than I thought there would be" Ma said. "Okay. We are now your guardians throughout this investigation. You will be allowed to stay with us until we determine what the best path is going forward for you" Pa said. Miles wanted to jump up and down and dance, but he restrained his excitement.

"Now let's get to the hospital" Pa said. Back in the car, Miles was thinking about how grateful he was that they are willing to help him. "Thank you for helping me" he said to both of them. "You are very welcome" Ma said. As they arrived at the hospital Pa said "here we are. Now let's understand something" he looked at Miles. "Based on the information Officer Bruce has provided, this little boy was not doing very well. If it turns out to be Willy, you need to stay calm and don't touch him. This little boy's injuries are really bad and the doctors are trying to figure out how they can help him. Do you understand?" Pa asked. "Yes sir" Miles said. "If you feel the need to get angry or throw a fit, go outside. Got it?" Pa finishes. "Yes sir" he responded. "Let's go inside" said Pa.

As they entered the hospital and passed the nurses desk, a lady at the desk welcomed them by saying "good morning Mr. Mayor." Pa looked up and said "good morning." As they continued down the hallway, another person said "good morning Mr. Mayor. I hope you are well this morning." Again and again people kept greeting him the same way. Miles looked up at Ma and said "why do they keep calling Pa Mr. Mayor? I thought his last name was Robinson, like yours." Ma smiled back at Miles and said "he is the Mayor of Little Elm, Miles." "What is Little Elm?" Miles asked.

Ma stopped and looked at him, questioning his question. "You don't know the name of the town you live in? The town is named Little Elm, son" she answered. "Oh" he said. "We never leave the trailer park, except to go to school. So I guess I never thought about the town name around us. No one had ever asked. So Pa is the Mayor. Well that explains why he has so many friends."

After a period of walking through the halls, they came to a nurse's desk and asked where the room was for the little boy that was brought in last night. The hospital named him 'John Doe' since he was not identified yet. Once Pa had the room number, he looked up and saw several police officers standing down the hall, including Officer Bruce. Pa turned and started to head towards them and Ma and Miles followed him.

Ma stopped Pa and said "hang on a second." She turned around and looked at Miles and said "are you ready for this?" He nodded his head and she said "just keep in mind, I will be right there with you if you need me." He reached out and took her hand. They started moving towards the room. As they approached, Officer Bruce walked up to them and said to Miles "now Miles, all I need you to do is take a look at him and tell me if you recognize him. Okay? It might not be real easy to tell if it is Willy or not because he has a lot of bandages on him. Okay?" "Okay" Miles said.

The police officers all moved to the side and let Officer Bruce lead Pa, Ma, and Miles into the room. Miles looked up and right away he knew it was Willy. Miles was still holding onto Ma's hand and was about to squeeze all the blood out of it. His heart was pounding and as he got closer to the bed, he could see his friend was really bruised a lot across his face.

They had a tube coming out of his mouth and on the opposite side, there were all sorts of wires hanging down from him. The machine behind him showed his current heart and breathing rates. Miles looked up at Pa and said with tears in his eyes "that's him. That's Willy. You can see his tattoo on his left arm. I put it there. Also, his hair is cut crooked on the left side, really chopped up. That's my step-mom's work."

Now with Willy identified and confirmed, Pa turned to Officer Bruce and nodded his head letting Officer Bruce know that this was indeed Willy as they had feared. As they were standing there, Miles looked back at Ma, who also had tears coming down her cheeks. Miles asked her "do you need to go outside Ma? I'll understand if you do. I need to stay and help Officer Bruce." She smiled and let go of his hand. You could see the marks on her hand where Miles had squeezed so hard. She left the room. Then Miles looked up at Pa and Officer Bruce and asked "now what happens?"

Officer Bruce looked at Pa and said "do you want me to tell him or do you want to?" Pa waved him on to go ahead. "Well, Miles our next move is to round up a group of officers and our CPS Manager, along with some forensics personnel, and go over to your home to have a talk with your family" Officer Bruce said.

"We are currently requesting a warrant to search the house and the shed. At the same time, we will be searching the property. We will need to gather as much evidence as we can to make an arrest, but we have to find enough proof for all of your allegations before we do so. We believe that Willy was hit by a car and left to die. As for you, Pa has mentioned you wanted to go with us. I think you may be of some help, but we have to have some ground rules. Okay?" "Okay" Miles answered.

"Pa, were you able to get the paperwork signed for Miles this morning?" Officer Bruce asked. "Yes, we also went ahead and filled out some paperwork for Willy as well, even though we did know if it was him yet. Now that we have confirmation that he is Willy, we are ahead of the game" Pa said. "This will allow us the legal right to deny the family access to your both" Pa explained.

"So Miles, one rule is that you are not to engage with anyone in your family" Officer Bruce said. "You need to let us do our job. You can only answer questions and engage with the officers. If they ask you a specific question, you are to give a specific answer. I know you are ten years old, but you seem pretty smart. I expect you to act that way while we are there." "Officer Bruce, I am sorry for busting your balls yesterday about not catching all of this before. I promise I will not get in your way. I do appreciate you letting me be involved in this. I have had to put up with the hatefulness of Willy's mom and my family ever since we moved into their house. I don't want them to get away with this anymore. So you can ask me anything and I will give you the truth" Miles said. "Pa, will you come to?" Miles asked. "Yes sir" Pa said.

After a plan was put together and the warrant was acquired, Pa explained to Ma the plan and asked if she wanted to come along. She said she wanted to stay at the hospital with Willy and wait until we got back. Ma turned and looked at Miles and said "Miles, I spoke with the doctor and they are going to take Willy in for surgery today. They hope to remove any broken and cracked rib bones, if they cannot be reset so that Willy can breathe better."

"If they can get his breathing to stabilize, they are going to bring in a specialist to work on his shoulder and hip injuries. I will keep you two informed as soon as I know how he does. Okay?" "Okay. Are we ready to go?" Miles asked. Officer Bruce looked over at Pa and said "I believe we have everything ready. Let's get going." Miles gave Ma a hug and turned and followed Pa and the rest of the officers outside.

Officer Bruce said to Pa "I don't think I have ever had to work with a ten year old before. This should prove to be interesting." "Well don't discount him because of his age" Ma said. "He is really bright and will surprise you" Pa responded. As they walked along, Pa wondered how any child could have been through what Miles had seen so far and turn out okay. This boy was tough he thought. Though I suspect by the end of all of this, he will need a lot of help.

Officer Bruce turned and said to Miles "your family hasn't called in a missing child yet. Do you think they will?" "No. As far as they are concerned, no one is missing. I think they did this to Willy. They don't believe anyone will miss him enough to care" Miles said. "Okay" said Officer Bruce.

Pa and Miles loaded up into the vehicle Officer Bruce was driving. It was not a normal police car. It was a big black cruiser with dark windows. Miles popped off "this is like a drug lord's car!" Pa started laughing. "What makes you say that Miles?" Pa asked. "Look at these windows. They are so dark, you can barely see out of them! I watch some TV shows" said Miles. "We use this vehicle for detective work, when they go out into the field to be undetected. You are correct, the windows make it hard to see inside" Officer Bruce responded.

As they drove along, it was quiet inside of the vehicle. Then the radio sounds startled Miles, as one of the officers in the group said to Officer Bruce that they were pulling into the trailer park. Officer Bruce responded "ten-four" he said. "We are just behind you. Don't approach the house until we get there." "Ten four" was the response.

Miles recognized the road at this point, and his heart began to race. He knew his family was going to be mad at him, especially coming in with the police. As they turned the corner into the trailer park, Miles told Officer Bruce to stop the car. As the vehicle came to a complete stop, Office Bruce looked back into the back seat at Miles.

Pa looked back and noticed that Miles had wet his pants. He had gotten so nervous, he didn't even know that had happened. His heart was racing really fast. He looked up at Pa and said "I don't know if I can do this. I am scared to death of these people! Oh my God, I wet my pants! Pa, what do I do?" Miles started to panic. "It going to be okay Miles" Pa said. "You and I will stay in the vehicle and let Officer Bruce and the rest of the police force handle this."

Miles was really upset now, he couldn't get calmed down. He knew he was about to let Officer Bruce down. "They need my help, but I can't!" "Miles" Officer Bruce looked right into his eyes. "It is going to be okay. I promise you we are not going to walk away empty handed. If I or one of my officers needs anything from you, we will come and ask you. Okay? So just sit tight and let us handle this." "Okay" Miles said. He sat back down and took deep breaths to help himself calm down. After all of this time, he didn't want to be the one reason they could not finish this job.

LIES UNSEEN – MARK WRIGHT

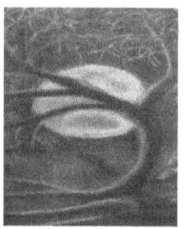

CHAPTER 5- A CLOSER LOOK

Officer Bruce pulled away and entered the trailer park. He parked his vehicle at the end of Miles's trailer home's drive and the rest of the vehicles parked at each corner of the trailer home. Officer Bruce stepped out of the vehicle and waved tohis lead officers to come over. He had set up three teams that included a lead officer with two junior officers and one forensic technician. Now he gave them instructions on what each group would do, as well as Jan Johnson, the CPS Manager. She would remain in the back at her vehicle until she was needed.

The first team was sent out to the edge of the field to find the tree Miles had said he and Willy had been tied to. At the same time, they were going to search the woods and creek bed for the items Miles said they had found. The second team was sent to concentrate around the outside parameter of the trailer home, which included the car and shed. The third team was going inside the house after the family was removed.

Officer Bruce was not sure how easy this investigation would be. All of the teams were to look for evidence of anything related to possible abuse or even attempted murder. Any evidence that backs up the stories told by Miles. On top of that, the team would inspect the house parameter and the only car in the driveway to see if it indicated any damage to it. They would also take samples, finger prints, blood, hair, and gather any suspicious evidence they might find.

Once everyone understood the plan, they were ready to go. Officer Bruce was ready to give the order to start. Then he stopped. He looked up and saw one of the neighbors walking his way, waving his arms then jogging towards them. As he approached, the neighbor said to the police officers "I think that car was in a hit and run accident. I heard them laughing and carrying on about it. But I noticed that both of the younger boys have not been home for at least two days." "Thank you" Officer Bruce said. "Now please go back to your home. If we need something else from you, we will come and get you." The neighbor looked like he wanted to stay, but went back to his home as Office Bruce requested.

Officer Bruce thought, shaking his head, why don't people ever come forward before it gets this bad? He didn't know. He turned around gave the order to the teams to start investigating. They began to approach the house and other areas assigned to them. As they approached the front door, it flew open. The officers stopped. Out the door stumbled an adult male, falling down the stairs. He appeared to be under the influence of some kind of intoxicant.

"Who is that?" he screamed. "Get your ass off my property!" he shouted. "It's the Little Elm Police Department sir" Officer Bruce announced. "We need you and your family to come out of the house, now please." "What the hell for? My whole family! I don't think so! Tell me why you're here" the man said.

Officer Bruce approached the house and began to talk with the man. "Sir, what is your name?" Officer Bruce asked. "Robert" he answered. "Robert who?" Officer Bruce asked. "Robert Dingwald" Robert said. "Now what is this all about?" he snapped.

"We have a warrant to search the premises and inside the house. We have reports of child neglect and abuse. Currently, we have one of your children that has been identified in the hospital for what appears to be from a hit and run car accident" Officer Bruce explained. "What?" Robert questioned. "One of my children! All of my kids are here, all present and accounted for! Here, let me get them out here."

"Marilyn, come out here and get all the kids out here!" Robert yelled. "These officers say we are being accused of… of… of, what was that again?" He looked back at Officer Bruce. Officer Bruce stated the charges again loud enough for Marilyn could hear them too. "Child abuse, neglect, and currently we have one of your children in the hospital from what appears to be a hit and run vehicular accident."

Marilyn stuck her head out the door and screamed "God dammit Robert! What the hell did you do this time?"

"Nothing! I have been here all day! Get those kids out here, so they can see everyone is fine." "Well...now...Willy and Miles aren't home, Robert" Marilyn said. "Well where the hell are they?" Robert asked. "They went over to their friend's house over at the other side of the park" Marilyn said.

About this time, Lewis walked out of the door and then came Rebecca. Carolyn came out next and then Jimmy. Jimmy looked up and said "that's not true. Neither one of those boys are anywhere near this park or trailer homes. You know that Momma! Miles ran away the day before yesterday, when we found them down at the river. Willy took off the same night after he showed us all that stuff they found. He took off when you, me, Lewis, and Rebecca were down at the river getting all of that stuff. Don't you remember? That bike over there, the dump truck, and that big ass TV in the living room." "Shut your pie-hole boy before I knock your head off!" Momma exclaimed.

Officer Green walked over and said something in Officer Bruce's ear. Officer Bruce walked over to the car and looked down. He could see blood all over the fender and the front right tire. He looked back and called Robert over to the car. "Robert, can you come over here please." Robert stumbled his way over. "Robert, do you see all of the red stuff there? Do you know what that is?" Officer Bruce asked. "Well...looks like some varmint blood. We have those all over here. We have a challenge to see who can hit the most" he laughed.

"Well, I will bet that blood is from your son Willy, who is in the downtown Little Elm hospital right now from possibly being hit by this car! We will be running some tests on this blood and it would be a smart move on your part to come clean now" Officer Bruce explained. "Clean about what? I haven't driven this car in at least three days!" Robert said.

Jimmy busted out laughing. "Boy, you guys are way off! That idiot wasn't driving the car! He stays so drunk, he can barely walk out the house much less drive!" "Shut your fucking mouth now!" Momma said. Jimmy looked at her and he knew she was serious. He also knew that he had to speak up. He knew that Miles and Willy were the cause of the police being here and it was finally time to tell the truth.

"What is your name son?" Officer Bruce asked. "Jimmy" he said. "Do you know who was driving this car?" he asked. Momma looked over at Jimmy with a look that she would kill him if he told the truth. But Jimmy just couldn't help himself. After all, she did tell him to do it.

All this time, he had been kissing her ass and now he could turn the tables. Jimmy grinned from ear to ear and said "yeah, I know who was driving and I know who was in the car. I was driving!" "How old are you boy?" Officer Bruce asked. "Twelve, almost thirteen" he replied. Marilyn's face was red and she looked like steam might come out her ears! Officer Green had to restrain her from interfering with Jimmy saying anymore.

"So tell me what happened Jimmy. How did you end up driving the car?" Officer Bruce pushed. Jimmy smiled and said "I got that little fucker! He took off the day before yesterday, close to sundown. Me and Momma loaded up in the car and took off after him. She told me it was my turn to drive. We knew he had gone out that way" as he pointed towards the road back to the right. "Miles had ran the other way, but I couldn't catch him. I wasn't going to let that happen twice!" Marilyn yelled "you little liar! He's lying! All lies!" Officer Green told her to shut up and quit struggling.

"We were driving down the main road when I saw Willy. Momma hollered 'hit that little Mother fucker! Run his ass over!' So I mashed on the pedal and off we went. He saw us coming too! That made it even more fun! Willy tried to run down into the woods, but I caught him just before he got there. Pop! I heard the right side of the car hit him and knock him down. I knew it was a good hit because the headlight broke out!"

"Momma hollered 'stop the car!' and she got out of the car. I couldn't see what she was doing. But I saw her raise her leg and step. She looked like she was holding him on the ground. I heard him screaming! It was awesome! We caught that bastard! Now, we are going to finish him! Momma told me to back the car up and turn the wheel, so I did. She told me to stop when the right front tire lifted off the ground. She was grinning from ear to ear" Jimmy said. "Then I heard a popping sound. That's when she got back into the car and told me 'let's go. This little fucker won't be problem anymore!'" As Jimmy finished his story, Officer Bruce heard someone behind him throwing up. He turned and saw that it was Officer Green.

Just as Officer Bruce turned back around Momma pulled out her whip from behind her back, the one that Miles had told him about. Only she had the butt end out. She escaped from Officer Green while he was throwing up and grabbed Jimmy by the hair and began pounding him across the head and his face! Officer Bruce jumped forward, along with two other officers, and grabbed her. They couldn't get her off of Jimmy.

Just about that time a pipe comes flying around like a baseball bat and hit her right in the back of the head. She fell backwards and hit the ground. Lewis was holding the pipe and screamed at her "stop it you crazy bitch! That's my brother you're hurting!" Then he threw the pipe on the ground. Rebecca turned around and grabbed Lewis by his groin and pushed him back into the trailer. He was screaming and trying to get away. Officer Green grabbed Rebecca by her collar and dragged her off of Lewis.

Jimmy fell over and had blood running out of the back of his head. You could see where Marilyn had hit him several times by the knots that the whip left on his head. However, Jimmy began to rise and turned with a huge smile on his face, laughing out loud, looking back at Marilyn. She was still on the ground dazed, but able to see what was going on.

"Remember the tongue!" Jimmy said. "You better remember the story you told me about how you got that tongue! Well now...it's my turn to be rewarded! All this time I have watched as you hurt my brothers! All this time we have sat back and watched as you swung that stupid whip! I've been waiting to tell the story of how you got that tongue! I knew my day would come to get you back for all the hurt you have caused us!" Jimmy spit at Marilyn and looked at her with hate in his eyes.

"Now you get your punishment, while I sit back and watch you rot!" Jimmy yelled "no one will touch me! No one will hurt me because of my age! I will walk the earth free from you and your insanity!" Officer Bruce yelled back at his officers and told them cuff both Marilyn and her daughter Rebecca. He said "put them in the squad cars and get me the medical kit. We need to stop Jimmy's bleeding. Then we are going to put him under arrest!" Jimmy said "me? You can't arrest me! I am only twelve years old!" he said to Officer Bruce. "You will be charged with attempted murder young man. I can arrest you and I am!" Officer Bruce said.

As the officers were cuffing the mother and daughter and placing them into the squad cars separately, they locked them in. Office Bruce turned and looked at the father, who was just staring at them in total fear. "Mr. Dingwald, I need to know what your involvement in this is. Did you know about them running over Willy?" "No" Robert responded "not at all." "Officer Green, did you find any evidence concerning the accusations about the children being locked up in the shed" Officer Bruce asked.

"Yes sir, we did. There is a chain welded to a post with a shackle attached to it inside the shed. Forensics found blood on the floor and the shackle. We have also found blood on the door at the opening. Looks like whoever was locked in there was trying to break out. The forensic techs will be testing the blood next to see if it is human" Officer Green said.

Officer Bruce turned around and looked at Mr. Dingwald. He looked confused. He said "that shackle was to hold the goat?" "We do not have a damn goat you fucking idiot!" Lewis screamed. "If you weren't drunk all the time, you would have known what she was doing!"

Officer Rice returned with her team and forensic officer from the field. She updated Officer Bruce letting him know that they had found the tree Miles had told them about. It had signs of blood all up and down its trunk. It also had a rope tied to its trunk. As for locating any of the stuff down by the river, nothing was found there.

Officer Bruce acknowledged he was aware of the items not being there, since they were here at the house. Officer Green showed Officer Bruce his handheld computer and that confirmed the stuff on the yard was in fact the stuff reported stolen just north of here. "Mr. Dingwald, are you aware that the items you have here at your home, like that bike, that dump truck, the tires, and the TV have all been reported as stolen by local families? What else do you have hidden here that might be necessary for us to investigate?" asked Officer Bruce.

"Uh… uh, what stuff are you talking about? We have one TV and it doesn't work half the time. I don't recall getting any of the kid's bikes. What dump truck?" Robert Dingwald asked. "Mr. Dingwald, can you not see the toys and tires next to your house? Are you not even aware of what is going on here? Maybe we can ask the children and see if they can help us" Officer Bruce said.

Mr. Dingwald looked over at Lewis who sighed and looked back at the Police officer. "Miles and Willy went down to the river to play the day before yesterday and found all of this stuff. Miles ran away, but Willy was caught. Willy, in an effort to save his ass, he told Mom so she wouldn't beat him. Mom had me, Rebecca, and Jimmy go down with her and collect it. We brought it all up from there" Lewis confessed. "We don't know how it got down there. All of it was brand new" Lewis continued. "Dad, of course, was drunk and passed out on the couch as usual" Lewis finished.

Officer Bruce wrote down what he was being told. "Did it occur to anyone to call the police?" he asked. Lewis laughed and said "yeah, right." "Okay with that said, you will be coming down to the station for an additional interview to make a statement in regards to your testimony. Got it?" Officer Bruce responded. Lewis nodded his head in agreement. "How old are you young man?" he asked. "Fourteen" Lewis said. Looking over at Officer Rice, Officer Bruce instructed her to "go ahead and put him in a police car alone. I am done with him for now. You can send the other two cars to the station to deliver the mother and daughter. Hold up on Lewis because we may need to bring the Dad in as well" Officer Bruce instructed Officer Rice. "Yes sir" she said.

After Jimmy was cleaned up and his wounds patched, the police decided to take him to the hospital for possible stitches. Officer Rice stopped Officer Bruce and asked what he wanted to do. They only had three vehicles and all three were being used. Two of them were sent back to the station with the other officers. "Go ahead and take Lewis and Jimmy in that car. On your way, call it in, and tell them we need at least one of the two cars to be returned. Preferably both" said Office Bruce.

While Officer Rice was busy coordinating the transportation of the family, Officer Green began gathering up the stolen items that were found all over the property. In the middle of his quest he stopped. He walked back over to Officer Bruce and spoke to him. "I think we may have another issue. Last month we had several complaints of tools, home gardening tools, and other outside items coming up missing."

"Nobody has been able to identify who took them or where they went to. Most of them were in an area just north of here" Officer Green said. Officer Bruce said "Okay, did you find something?" "Yes, I would say so. Come with me" he responded. As they walked around the back, Officer Green pointed to an opening in the back of the trailer thathe had noticed on his second trip around it.

When he pulled back the trailer skirting, they found a whole new treasure trove of items that might be the stolen tools. The officer assisting Officer Green had removed a pile of tools, tool boxes full of tools, gardening tools, and a host of miscellaneous tools used to work around the house. Further under the house, they pulled out three lawn mowers and one tiller. Officer Bruce instructed one of the officers to call the police station and see if they could bring the two ton truck out here. He turned and said "good find, Officer Green. I guess we need to go arrest the rest of the family and see if we can sort all this out at the station."

Officer Bruce walked back around the front and called Officer Rice over and asked if she had been able to get in touch with the station about another car. "Yes sir, I was able to reach the junior officer driving a car. They have dropped off the daughter and mother and both cars are on their way back here" she said. "Okay, well let's go ahead and arrest the father as well" he said.

"Mr. Dingwald, are you going to stand here and pretend you had no idea about all of the alleged abuse that was going on in your family? You had no idea about all of these stolen items and how they ended up here on your property? Along with a large list of stolen items we just removed from under your home? You are telling me you know nothing about any of it? Mr. Dingwald I am sorry but I find it hard to believe you are completely innocent" Officer Bruce exclaimed. "I didn't say that" Mr. Dingwald responded.

"Because of all the evidence we have uncovered so far, we are going to place you under arrest with the rest of the family. This will all be sorted out at the station. CPS will be taking your youngest girl. Young lady, what is your name?" Officer Bruce asked. "Carolyn" she said. "How old are you?" he asked. "I am nine years old" she said. "Well Carolyn, we are going to have to take your Mom and Dad down to the police station. This nice lady here is named Mrs. Johnson and she is going to take you with her for now" Officer Bruce explained to her.

Carolyn looked up and smiled at Mrs. Johnson and said "am I going to live with you?" Mrs. Johnson was a woman of about five foot three inches tall. She has blonde hair and blue eyes with a very soft look and small smile. She leaned over to Carolyn and said "well maybe not live with me, but how about you stay with me awhile?" "Okay" Carolyn said.

Carolyn looked back at her father and said "bye Daddy, I love you." As Carolyn and Mrs. Johnson walked towards her car, Officer Bruce looked around to see the evidence they have gathered up so far. Tree blood and evidence of physical abuse at the tree; multiple items stolen from local families; blood inside the shed and evidence of someone inside possibly trying to break out.

Officer Bruce walked into the house while his third team was still working inside the house. This team was put together with two forensic technicians and one junior officer. They were all working diligently to find as much evidence as possible. Officer Bruce talked to the junior officer and said "let's do a good sweep inside. Find any evidence and take samples, but I think we are going to find most of the evidence outside."

"Do you want us to assist one of the other teams?" the junior officer asked. "Not yet, just keep going with what you are. Give the inside a good going over and gather whatever you can find. If we need you outside, we will let you know" Officer Bruce said. He turned and walked back out the front door and looked across the horizon. Noticing a sudden level of darkness; not because of the time but because of the dark nature of this investigation. He never expected to find any truth to what Miles had told him and was really disturbed and disgusted about it.

He gathered his teams and they began to devise a further plan on how to proceed going forward. Officer Bruce talked to Officer Green and Officer Rice individually. He wanted them to stick around and lead the investigation. Based on the information they have found so far, he told them to not leave any stone unturned. Make sure they went back down by the river and checked for any other items or evidence. They needed to walk the property and knock on the doors of neighbors, canvasing the area. They needed to assist the techs in the house and look for anything that could lead to a possible conviction.

Officer Bruce explained to the officers "I have never seen anything this bad and I don't want to let these people get away. We need all the evidence we can get. Also, make sure you look for this so called tongue. I am curious as to what that is all about."

"Oh, we found that earlier. It was hanging right in the living room on the wall" said Officer Green. "We were not sure what it was at first but then one of the forensic techs reminded us about what the boy had said." He walked over and picked up a plastic bag with the tongue in it and handed it to Officer Bruce. Inside was a picture frame with a tongue nailed to the back plate. At the bottom of the frame was a gold plated sign that read 'Daddy.' "What the hell is that?" Officer Bruce asked. "Not sure, but we are going to have it tested" the tech said. "It looks like a human tongue" he continued.

"I need to get back to the station, so we can start interviewing the family and see if we can make any sense of all of this. I have to drop off Mayor Robinson and Miles so that they can visit Willy at the hospital. I will check on Willy, who was gravely injured when a car ran over him while I drop them off. Make sure we didn't miss any family members beside the youngest girl who went with Mrs. Johnson. You two officers watch over this investigation here and let me know if you need anything. Use all of our resources, whatever you need" Officer Bruce said.

"If you need more officers, we can recruit from the City of Paxle. I am friends with the Mayor over there as well" said Officer Bruce. He then turned and saw a junior officer standing right behind him, looking like she wanted something. "Officer Michele, how can I help you?" Officer Bruce asked.

"That neighbor that came over earlier is back and he said he had some more information for you" she said. "Lord what now! Does this mess have an end to it? What could he possibly have that could make this any worse? Did you ask him?" he asked her. "Yes sir, but he was adamant that he only wanted to talk to you" she answers. "Okay, but Officer Rice, you are coming with me. I may need a witness" he said.

They turned around and walked down past the cars over to the field. The neighbor standing there was a short, fat, and appeared to be an older man. His head was mostly bald and he stood there with his pants barely held up without a belt. His shirt was a white tank top that didn't cover his large, lower belly. As Officer Bruce got closer and the man started walking in his direction. Suddenly, Miles and Pa stepped in front of Officer Bruce looking as if they wanted to know what was going on.

Officer Bruce put his hand up and told Officer Rice to let the neighbor know he would be there shortly. "Guys…I have not forgotten about you, but we have a lot of stuff going on here. As soon as I am done with this guy, we are going to leave and I will explain what has happened so far. Fair enough?" Officer Bruce told them. "That's James Bufford, our neighbor or nosy neighbor as Mom always called him" Miles said. Pa looked at him with concern. "We okay?" he asked. "Yes" Officer Bruce responded. "Let me deal with this guy first."

Officer Bruce walked over to James Bufford and said "how can I help you Mr. Bufford?" "How do you know my name?" he asked. "I don't think that is really important, now is it?" Officer Bruce asked. "I guess not" Mr. Bufford responded. "Now back to how can I help you. What information do you have that I may need that is pertinent to this case?" Officer Bruce asked.

"You know that woman over there grew up here in this trailer park. She lived here as a child. Her Mother left her and her father alone together when she was young. Her father disappeared one day when she was about twelve years old. We all thought she had killed him, but the police could never find his body. They assumed he left her like her Mother had" Mr. Bufford began. "So the police took her away and put her in the system."

"Mr. Bufford, may I ask what does this have to do with this case?" Officer Bruce asked. "Well" he said. "They took her away when all that happened and she returned to this trailer when she was around eighteen years old. Since her mother and father owned the plot of land and home, she moved back in. She has been married several times. Most of them just leaving after a short while. One of them just disappeared because we never saw him leave. I have noticed that she had a real fondness for that tree right out there in the field, next to where the river drops off."

"You mean where she has been beating those children?" Officer Bruce asked. "Oh, she only beat two of the boys over there. I never saw her with any of the other kids out there" Mr. Bufford said. "Where is this going Mr. Bufford? I have a long night ahead of me and I don't have time for a nosy neighbor who only wants to tell rumors after the fact" Officer Bruce getting impatient.

"I am sorry Officer. We should have said something years ago. We don't like to stick our noses in other people's business. If we are right in what we suspect, we would be in the same place as her father was. I think you need to have your officers take a closer look around that tree. Maybe dig a hole or two to investigate it more?" Mr. Bufford said.

"You think the father and one of her husbands are buried there?" "Yes" "You should have come forward a long time ago with this information. Especially for those children. Go home Mr. Bufford and we will look into it. One of our officers will be by later to talk with you more" Officer Bruce said angry at this point. Mr. Bufford hung his head down, turned around, and headed back to his house.

Officer Bruce turned and looked at Officer Rice and before he could say anything she said "I will get some of the officers back to the tree and take another look. I bet you wished we had a few detectives at this point, don't you?" "It would certainly make our jobs easier. Now, we have our entire police force on this one case trying to gather evidence. I think I am going to call Mayor Rogers over in the City of Paxle and get some of his people over here as well" Officer Bruce said.

"This is a lot to have to keep track of. I need to talk to both you and Officer Green again before I leave. What is really sad is we were just here last week, looking into the boy that is in the hospital. Had we paid closer attention, we would have caught all of this then. Damn this is a bad deal!" Officer Bruce said.

"Well it doesn't help that the neighbors have been watching this go on for all this time and said nothing. Is it possible to arrest some of them as well?" Officer Rice asked. "Let's just stick to what we have so far. If we determine that they were involved or neglected to do their civic duty, we will see" Officer Bruce responded. "I will be over at my car talking to Mayor Robinson and Miles, the other little boy. I need to give them an update. Can you round up Officer Green and bring him over to me?" he requested. "Yes sir" she responded.

Officer Bruce walked back over to his car and opened the door. Taking a long moment, he sat down inside the vehicle and started to give both Pa and Miles an update. Pa stopped him and said "we watched it all from here. I cannot believe that little boy admitted to running over Willy. I am also shocked about all the stuff you have been finding. I stopped Officer Rice on the way in from the river and we talked about what she had found out there. It is really upsetting! According to Miles, you have found more stuff then even he knows nothing about."

Since they had watched from the car, Officer Bruce had no reservations about asking Miles any questions at this point. He turned to Miles and asked about the tongue in the frame. "Mom told us this story. When she was a little girl, her dad was trying to physically do things to her she didn't want him to do. One night she waited until he went to sleep and she cut out his tongue. She said later that he made such a mess bleeding everywhere, she just cut off his head. She burned the body and scattered his ashes and parts all over the field out back behind the house. She buried his head up by the tree along with a few other unlucky gentlemen she said. She put his tongue in that frame as a reminder. We always thought it was made up story. Just to scare us" Miles said. "It obviously didn't work or we wouldn't be here now" Miles finished.

Officer Green and Officer Rice arrived at the car and Officer Bruce excused himself so he could talk to them. "Listen, this case is quite difficult for all of us and I need to make sure both of you are on board and can keep your heads on straight. We cannot afford to ruin any of the evidence here. So, I need you to really make a good choice. I know this is hard and I also know that you are both trained for this. We cannot afford to contaminate any evidence. No one will fault you if you decide you need to leave. I brought both of you here because you are the best officers in our group and I believe we can make a really strong case against these criminals. Again, this is one of the toughest cases any of us have ever had. So I need you to think about it and let me know that you are onboard, okay?" Officer Bruce explained.

"I know what this about and I am really sorry about that. I just lost it when the boy was telling us how they ran him over. It just hit me so hard!" Officer Green said. "I am fine now. I am not willing to leave at this point because we need to take down this family. All of them. I can do my part Officer Bruce" Officer Green continued. "I am good" Officer Rice said thumbs up. "Okay, well Officer Rice now has a new task concerning the tree to handle. Let me know if anything comes of that" Officer Bruce said.

"I am going to call Mayor Rogers over at the City of Paxle and have some of his officers come run our station to assist us there. I believe the forensic crew we have will be able to gather any evidence that we need. Officer Green, please keep working the grounds here at the house and assist with the inside investigation as well. We don't know what evidence we will find, so we need to expect anything. We need this to be by the book, everything by the book. Make sure you log everything. Let me know what you find and I will see you all back at the station later. Thank you" Officer Bruce completed.

As the officers turned towards their respective tasks, Officer Bruce took a deep breath and climbed into his vehicle. He turned and could see Miles staring at him. Miles said "thank you. You have no idea how much this means to me and Willy. Are we going back to the hospital now?" Miles asked. "Yes" Officer Bruce responded.

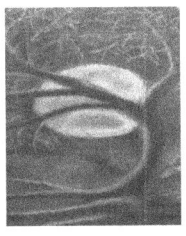

CHAPTER 6- NEW HOPE

"Okay...okay, I understand. Yes, we are about to leave. I will let him know" Pa said on the phone. "Well" he said after he hung up the phone. "It seems that Willy is a pretty tough boy. He made it through the surgery and the doctors said they had to remove three of his ribs and replace them with some new synthetic material. They were able to repair the rest. His breathing has improved and his heart rate is back down. He is still not awake but they are hopeful he will wake up soon. He is in the Intensive Care Unit (ICU) and they are waiting for him to stabilize once his status has improved. Once he wakes up, they will continue caring for him from there. Additional surgery will be needed but Willy has a long road to go until he is well enough to return to normal."

As they headed back to the hospital, Officer Bruce explained to Pa and Miles about all of the things they had found so far. Miles said "wait...what stuff is under the house? I never knew anything about all of that! How did it get there?" "We do not know. It doesn't appear anyone will be forthcoming with that information. We have taken your father, Lewis, Rebecca, and Jimmy to the station for questioning. Of course, that is after Jimmy is done at the hospital" said Officer Bruce. "Our hopes are that we can get at least one of them to open up and give us some information."

"According to your neighbor Mr. Bufford, your mother spent a lot of time around that tree she whipped you boys at. He suspects there are some bodies buried there." "Huh!" Miles retorted. "That would explain a lot. She used to sneak out at night with a couple of candles and go to that tree. She wouldn't come in for a long time."

"Me and Willy went out there one time we wanted to try to dig something up, to see what she was hiding. Jimmy was watching us so we had to get out of there. If she found out what we were planning, I am pretty sure we would be buried there too!" Miles said.

"I have a couple of officers checking into the tree area more as we speak. Based on what we have seen so far, there is no telling what they will find. As for the stuff under the house, are you sure you have no idea what is down there?" Officer Bruce asked Miles. "No, I have no idea what is down there. I also don't know how it got there. We just found the stuff at the river yesterday and we been down there all the time. So whoever put it there, did it recently. I still don't understand why they would throw away such good stuff!" Miles said. Officer Bruce looked up to watch Miles' response, seeing if he can see any signs he may be lying. Deep into the back of his mind, he thought that Miles had some element of involvement in all of this.

As they turned into the parking lot at the hospital, Miles stomach began to turn. He knew they said Willy was doing better, but he was still scared. Scared his friend would not get out of the hospital alive! He was angry that his stepmother and brother did this to him! He was angry that his father drinks so much and doesn't pay any attention to what is going on! Miles knew that his father was only married his stepmother because he needed someone to watch his children. He believed that if he wasn't drinking all the time, he would see all the terrible things she was doing.

After they parked the car, Pa turned around and looked back at Miles. "Miles" he said. "Keep in mind that you can't touch him yet because of all of his injuries. Ma said they would explain to us about his shoulder and hip injuries when we get in there, okay?" "Okay" Miles responded. They got out of the car and went inside the hospital. They walked through the halls and back to the room where Willy currently is in. Ma was sitting in the room next to Willy as they walked up.

Ma came out and gave Miles a big hug. She turned to Pa and gave him one as well. She smiled at Miles and Pa and pulled them to the side to talk. "Good thing we went ahead and had the paperwork done on Willy this morning. Otherwise, I would not be able to tell you anything. They were reluctant on giving me any information earlier until I showed them those forms due to some HIPPA rules and such. The doctor said he will come to us soon and provide us with a complete update" she said.

"Since his surgery, his breathing has improved immensely. His other injuries are doing okay, but those injuries are going to require a specialist to fix them" she continued. "The doctors are monitoring him and hope that he will wake up soon. If he does from what the nurse said, it will make any other surgeries easier" Ma finished.

"Can I go in and see him?" Miles asked. "Yes" she said. "There is a chair you can sit in and talk to him if you want to. I don't know if he can hear anything, but I believe it is comforting."

Miles stepped into the room leaving both of them in the hallway. Miles heard Ma ask Pa "how is he doing?" "Well, after everything we just went through, a lot better than I would be doing. They unraveled a whole host of stuff today and it is still growing. It's possible that the mother has someone buried on that property too!" he said.

"Oh my God!" she said "Who do they think it is?" "From the story she told the kids, she may have cut out her father's tongue and then cut off his head. Also a couple of her husbands disappeared without a trace" Pa said. "Then the second oldest boy admitted to running down Willy with the car and the mother was with him. The story he told us was horrifying! I have never seen anything like this and I am sure it will only get worse! They have arrested practically the whole family, except for these two and the smallest daughter. She went with CPS. I am hoping Officer Bruce can build a good case and get some real answers."

Ma just stood there with her hand over her mouth in total shock at this latest revelation. It's horrible she thought! These poor children, having to endure this with no one there to stop it! As she stood there, Willy's doctor began walking towards her. She turned to Pa and pointed to him. "That is Willy's doctor" she said.

Pa looked over at Miles in the room and was about to call him over. Ma stopped him, so that they could talk to the doctor first. "Hello" the doctor greeted them. "My name is Dr. George. I performed Willy's surgery today and am here to answer any questions you might have. I have been working with the physicians and staff caring for Willy. My understanding is you are the Mayor? I have also been told you and your wife have accepted guardianship of Willy?" he said. "Yes I am and my name is James Robinson. Yes, we had the papers signed this morning to have guardianship over Willy, knowing that he would need someone to take care of him" Pa said.

"What can you tell me about his condition?" Pa asked. "Well as you probably are aware, we completed a procedure to open up his chest and remove the ribs that were broken and not repairable. Some of the damaged ribs had to be replace with a new synthetic bone material. The others we were able to repair. As of right now, our intentions are to allow him heal for at least twenty four hours more. We will wait to see if he wakes up in that timeframe" the doctor explained.

"If he does wake up, then the next step will be much easier. We have two specialist on call, ready to start the procedures on repairing both of Willy's hip and shoulder joints. They will reset his humorous bone at the same time.

This will be performed in two separate surgeries. Both within a few days of each other" Doctor George continued.

"What if he does not wake up in the next twenty four hours?" Pa asked. "If he doesn't, that will cause us to move a lot slower. These procedures require specialized anesthesiologists that can manage his breathing while he is under. Either way, we will have to address both injuries simultaneously. He could lose a leg or arm if he is unable to heal properly. We prefer to avoid that" the doctor responded.

"Do you have any personnel watching over him to see when he wakes up or do we need to do shifts ourselves to help? I am sure that young boy in there would be willing to stay all night if needed. Both Ma and myself as well" Pa said.

"Let's check at the nurse's station and see how their staffing situation is. We can always use an extra set of eyes" the doctor said. As they walked over to the nurses' station, Ma reached out and took Pa's hand into her own. She was reminded of one of the reasons she loved this man so much. He just agreed to take in two children that were not their own and he was willing to treat them as if they were welcome and care for them.

"This is Nurse Karen" Dr. George said. "She is the head nurse in this department. Karen, this is Mayor Robinson and his wife. I am sorry, I guess I never got your name?" Doctor George said. "Mattie Robinson" Ma said.

"Mattie" he shook her hand. "Karen, we were wondering if the staffing situation was strong enough to watch over the young boy in room 314 continuously or do you need some assistance? I believe if I understood them correctly, the Robinsons were willing to assist?" Doctor George asked.

"We always welcome help if we can get it. Tonight, we are fully staffed and I intend to place both Roberta and Carla on that side of the hall to make sure we were able to check on Willy frequently" nurse Karen responded.

"Okay" Doctor George said as he looked back at Ma and Pa. "It is up to you how you want to proceed, though it sounds like we have Willy covered tonight." Pa looked over at Ma and said "I am really beat after everything I have seen today. Let's go home and get some rest. Miles can come home as well with us. We will plan to come back in the morning first thing. Can you please call us if there is any change in Willy's condition, no matter what time it is?" Pa asked the nurse. "Of course Mr. Mayor" Nurse Karen responded.

Both Ma and Pa walked into Willy's room and saw Miles sitting next to him, talking to Willy. "Is he responding?" Ma asked. "No ma'am" Miles said. "We are going to go home, so we can get some rest. We want you to come with us and we can come back in the morning to see Willy. The hospital has a full staff and they plan to have two nurses watching over him closely tonight. They will call us and let us know if any changes occur in the night" Ma said to Miles.

"Can't I stay here tonight?" Miles asked. "Well...we talked about that and we think it would be better if you came with us to get some rest. It has such a crazy day, with all that has happened. It will allow us to refresh ourselves and come back in the morning to see Willy. Then we can talk to Willy's doctor about his plans for him" Ma said. "Okay" Miles responded. He reached out and touched his brother's hand. "Hang in there little brother. I am really sorry this happened to you" Miles said. As they left the room, Miles looked back one more time, hoping that Willy would wake up before he left.

On the way home, Ma explained to Miles what the doctor had told them. Miles just sat back and listened. He wondered if all of this would help get his stepmother and his father what they had coming to them, along with Jimmy and Rebecca. Almost every day since they became a family, there had been some sort of angry outburst happening. Miles and Willy were caught in the middle of it, getting punished.

Now…little Willy has been hurt really bad and Miles wanted to make sure that those assholes were punished for what they have done to them! What Miles realized was that before he came to live with Willy, he was alone dealing with his family. He didn't want to lose Willy.

When they arrived at the house, Ma went in to start dinner. Pa turned and said to Miles "come with me son." "Where?" Miles asked. "We need to get the horses back into the barn and feed the cows" Pa said. "Horses, cows, pigs, and chickens? You have a lot of animals to take care of" Miles said. "Yep" Pa said. They headed out the back door and onto the back porch. As they walked towards the barn, Miles could see a deer eating the grass inside the fence. "Hey look!" he said. "There is a deer over there!" "Yep" Pa said. Well, that was new. Miles had never seen an actual deer in real life until now. What a pretty animal he thought.

They had arrived at the barn and Pa pulled a harness off the wall and handed it to Miles. "Take this harness with us. We have two horses we need to corral and put in the barn. Now they might be a little rowdy, so don't step in front of them or they will run you over" Pa said to Miles. "Are any of your animals nice? You have pigs that will eat kids, chickens that will bite my fingers off, and now horse's that wants run me down! I hope your cows have a little less of an angry streak!" Miles said. Pa just laughed as they walked towards the pen.

"Alright. Now I will place the harness on his neck and you can hold the reins" Pa instructed Miles. "Reins…what is that?" Miles asked. "This" Pa raised the reins up and handed the long strands of leather straps to Miles. "Just stand back here and let me get him set up. He is going to be a little restless at first, but we will calm him down. Then you can take him into the barn and put him in one of the horse stalls. Then we will come back and get the next one" Pa said.

As Miles stood there holding the reins, he could not help but notice the size of this animal. His head was bigger than Miles leg! He was brown all over and had a lock of hair around his neck that was almost blonde colored. His back appeared to be slightly taller than Miles. And the top of his head was almost as tall as Pa! Pa reached out and placed the harness over the horse's head.

Miles held onto the reins and stood back to the side of the horse. As Pa placed the harness around his neck, Miles noticed that the horse seemed to not like it at all. He jumped and shook his head back and forth pretty forcibly. Pa stepped back and let him calm down, then went at him again. The second time Pa was able to get the harness onto the horse's neck. He attached the clasp and pulled the harness tight. "Okay" Pa said. "Let's give him a tug and let him know who the boss is."

Miles pulled on the reins and the horse pulled back, almost pulling Miles off the ground but not quite. Pa grabbed Miles and held him in place and told him to pull again. He did and this time the horse didn't move. "Off we go" Pa said. Miles stayed slightly to the left of the horse as they began to walk towards the gate. The horse was still trying to pull back against the reins, but Pa reached over and tugged the reins hard. Then the horse began to move forward. Slowly at first the horse allowed Miles to lead him to the gate and into the barn. Pa went around and opened the gate to his stall and the horse went into it.

Inside the stall was lots of hay and a trough. The stall was built out of wooden boards that went side to side. The stall was big enough for the horse to move around in and sleep. The trough had some feed in it already. Pa then removed the harness from the horse and closed the stall's gate. Then they went back to the pen for round two with the second horse. "Good job Miles! You were made for this" Pa said. After the second horse was placed into the barn, it was time to feed the cows. As they went out to the silo to get some feed, Miles noticed that there were no cows to be seen.

"Pa where are the cows? How are we going to feed them if they are not here?" Miles asked. "You'll see" Pa said. They filled up a wheel barrow with feed and Pa grabbed two big buckets. He raised the wheel barrow's handles so that only the wheels were touching the ground and started walking towards the fence line. When they were at the fence, Pa walked over to a big bell hanging on a post and grabbed the rope and began to ringing the bell. He rang it about three times. Then Pa came back over and handed Miles a bucket. "See those troughs over there? Fill this bucket and put three full buckets in each one of the troughs" he told Miles.

Just as Miles began to pour his first bucket of feed, he could hear the sound of rumbling and mooing from the distance. He looked up and the cows were running over the horizon coming towards the fence. "You need to hurry up son. When they get here, they are going to be hungry!" Pa said. "They are not going to eat me are they?" Miles asked. "They might take a hand if you don't hurry!" Pa said. Miles was hustling to get the feed into each of the troughs. Lucky for him, he realized Pa hadn't opened the gate to allow them in to eat until after he was done.

The cows herded over to the troughs, and like big dogs, they just put their heads inside the troughs and started huffing and eating. Shaking their heads and sucking in the feed. Pa grabbed the wheel barrow and pushed it back into the barn, then they started walking towards the house. Pa told Miles to go wash up and get ready for dinner. As Miles walked into the back room of the house where he slept the night before, he noticed a new set of clothes laid out for him to wear. There was also a pair of pajamas and he thought wow! I don't believe I have ever had a pair of pajamas before or clean clothes every day! He went into the bathroom and took a shower. After cleaning up, he put on the pajamas and headed into the kitchen. Of course, he had to find it first.

"Oh…you already showered?" Ma said. "Yes Ma'am" Miles said. "Pa told me to clean up for dinner." "Well, I think he meant to wash your hands so you could eat. But a shower works too" Ma responded with a grin. "Oh" Miles said. "How does chicken sound for dinner? "Ma asked. "Great! I am so hungry I could eat a horse!" Miles said. "Hey watch out now, we ain't cooking up any of my horses" Pa grinned as he entered the room. "Got some of that world class sweet tea Ma?" he asked. She pointed to the counter where she had already poured him a glass.

Ma was finished cooking and placed everything into large bowls. The chicken was placed on a plate and everything moved to the table. "Oh my God!" Miles said. "You people eat like Kings!" There was so much food. At his house, they never had meals like this. Usually, one item was made or microwaved, and that's it! All of them had to share what was on the table. Right now he is looking at ten of his normal home meals.

Miles reached over and got some mashed potatoes, and Ma handed him the gravy. "What's that for?" he asked. "Your potatoes" she said. "Is it good?" Miles asked. Pa looked up and said "the best." Miles took the spoon and put a small bit of gravy onto his mashed potatoes. Then Ma passed him the chicken plate. There must have been a dozen chicken pieces on this plate. Legs, thighs, and breasts all on one plate. He really wasn't sure how to recognize one piece of chicken from another. So he just reached over and took the one that looked the best. Then Ma passed the green beans to him. Miles looked down and he didn't have any room left on his plate. "I will get some of these beans later. I have to make a spot for it" Miles said.

"Make a spot" Pa said. "Just pile it next to something else. It all goes to the same place" he said. "Leave him be" Ma said. "If he needs to make a spot, let him make a spot" she continued. Then Ma passed the rolls over and Miles took one of them. He set it next to his plate on his napkin. He didn't know where to start eating, so he started with the roll. Pa looked up and said "try it with your potatoes, just dip it like this" as he dipped his roll into his mashed potatoes and took a big bite. "Pa, just let the boy eat however he wants. If he doesn't want to mix his food, he doesn't have too!" Ma said.

As Miles ate, he watched as both Ma and Pa mixed the food together. He had always been this way. He hated his foods mixed. His brothers and sisters always made fun of him because of it. Sometimes they would mix his food on his plate just to mess with him. Always making him feel different because of who he was. Of course, he always told himself they were jealous because he was so much smarter. Miles liked to believe he was in the wrong family. That the doctors dropped him off at the wrong house. There was no way he could be a part of that group of idiots.

Once dinner had ended and Miles had survived Pa's antics, he helped Ma clear the table and wash the dishes. He told Ma thank you for the day and he thought he should go ahead and get some sleep. As he was heading back to the room he was in last night, Ma stopped him and said "you are going to be okay, Miles." "Also, you are not staying in the room you were in last night. I had the maid clean out another room for you. You can stay there until we determine what is going to happen long-term. So, let me take you back there and show you where you will be sleeping" she finished.

As they were walking through the halls, Pa hollered out to Miles "be ready to get up early in the morning. We have to do some extra chores tomorrow." "Yes sir" Miles said. Ma led Miles down a couple of hallways and then through two rooms; one room had a pool table in it and the other room had a great big fireplace. They passed through these rooms and then went up a set of stairs. Miles thought to himself, I am going to have to eat again by the time we find this room. At the top of the stairs they came to a small room. She entered it and showed him the closet. "The bathroom is down the hall. You can stay here until we figure things out. Okay?" she asked. "Okay, thank you" Miles said.

"Goodnight" Ma said as she went back down the stairs. Miles looked out the window. He could see all the way out to the furthest side of the property or at least that's what he thought he was looking at. It was getting dark outside and he just stood there in amazement. How do people live like this? They have to be rich! Look at all that land! All of the animals they have and they feed them too! Hell at Miles house, they couldn't even feed the feral cats! Of course, his stepmom would shoot them whenever she saw them.

As Miles settled down to bed, he realized that this had been a very long day. He realized that even though he lived in the same house with the rest of his family, he did not know a lot of what was going on there. He fell asleep recounting the day's events. Next thing he knew, the sun was coming into his window and he could hear Pa hollering from downstairs for him to get up. He looked out the door and waved at Pa. "Get dressed Miles. We have to get an early start today" Pa said. Miles turned around and rubbed his face. Man these people get up early every day!

Miles sat down on the bed and thought about how he had imagined his life changing when he left that house. Not one time did he see himself sleeping in a house like this one. Most of his dreams had him and Willy traveling as far away as possible. Foraging for food and fighting society to stay alive. How he could conjure up a scheme to entrap his family, so they would be punished for their crimes. He always played the hero in his dreams. Turns out, there are no heroes he decided. Just good people, trying to do the right thing.

He looked over and noticed that Ma must have been in the room sometime in the night because the clothes were laid out for him in the other room were sitting on the chair in this room. This time, he noticed a pair of sneakers next to the clothes. He got up and put the clothes on, but instead of the sneakers, he put on the boots. He knew Pa was going to take him to the barn and he didn't want to get these new sneakers dirty. He began the trek down to the kitchen. It took a while, but he finally found the kitchen. Pa was already at the table eating a plate full of food.

Pa looked up and said "good morning. Hope you had a good night's rest." "Yes sir, I did" Miles said. "You said last night that we had more chores to do today before we go to the hospital. Like what?" Miles asked. "Well to start with, we have to clean the horse manure out of the stalls. Then we need to feed the pigs and chickens again like we did yesterday" Pa said. "So the only new thing is taking horse poop out of the horse stalls?" Miles asked. "Yes, that is the only new thing" Pa said somewhat irritated at Miles attitude.

Miles made himself a plate with a couple of eggs, bacon, and one biscuit. Today he noticed that Ma had made more gravy. So, he put some more of that gravy on his plate. While he was eating, Pa reached over and tapped Ma on her shoulder. She turned around and Miles was dipping his biscuit in the gravy and stuffing it in his mouth.

Ma said "how is the gravy today?" "Oh, it's really good especially if you mix it with the biscuit!" he said. Ma just smiled.

Once Miles had finished his meal, he got up and went over to the sink. Ma said "just put your dishes in the sink. I will clean them later." Miles thanked Ma and headed out to the barn where he thought Pa was. When he got out there, he found Pa wasn't there. Miles looked around and saw two really big forks sitting in the hay. He grabbed one and went over to the stall and opened the gate. As he was opening the gate, the horse charged towards him. He slammed the gate shut! The horse ran into it and stepped back.

Miles tried to open it again but the horse charged again. About that time Pa hollered "wait a minute son! Don't open that gate or that horse will run you down! He wants to get out to the mare over there. She is in heat and he wants to get to her. If you let him loose, none of us could settle him down! That's why we are going to move him out into the field first. Then the other horse next to him can go out to the field." Pa reached up on the post and grabbed this horse's harness.

He reached over the side of the stall and made a clicking sound with his mouth. The horse walked over to him and Pa took the harness and put it onto the horse's neck. He then told Miles to open the gate. As Miles opened the gate, he stepped into the stall with the horse who was very agitated. Once Pa had the harness tight on the horse, he jerked down on the reins to settle him down. Then pulled him out of the stall and headed the horse towards the field. He released that horse by taking off his reins, then they went back to the barn to clean out his stall and deal with the next horse.

After Miles had removed all of the horse poop in both stalls, they threw in a bale of hay into each stall. Pa used a pair of wire cutters to cut the wire off each bale of hay. Miles then spread the hay all over each stall. Miles learned that a bale of hay was quite heavy. Then Pa moved the second horse to the first horses stall. They repeated this for the third horse. The last one was also taken to the field to join the first one. Miles was now about worn out. Pa smiles and said "we need to feed the chickens and pigs now." "Yeah, yeah, yeah" Miles responded.

He turned around and looked at Pa and said "what does in heat mean?" "They don't teach you the birds and the bees in school boy?" Pa asked. "I guess not" Miles said. "Well hell!" Pa said. "They are just ruining schools these days! All the simple things in life and they can't talk about them anymore! You see that horse over there in that barn?" Pa asked, pointing to the second barn. "Yes" Miles said.

"Well, those two horses out there are boy horses and that one in there is a girl horse. That girl has a certain smell to her that will drive those boys crazy when she is in heat. They want to make her their girlfriend. Do you understand?" Pa asked. "So far, I think" Miles answered. "We have to keep those horses far enough away from each other, so that they can't smell her. Otherwise, they will hurt themselves or anything in their path to get to her" Pa continued. "Is this a sex talk, like when I caught Rebecca and Lewis in the barn?" Miles asked. "Excuse me?" Pa asked.

"I left my basketball at the old barn just outside our trailer park. I went back to get it one day and saw Rebecca and Lewis having sex. Or at least that's what I thought it was. They both had their pants off and she was on his lap" Miles told Pa. Pa just stared stunned and said "Yes, this is a sex talk. What did you do?" Pa asked. "Are you kidding? I snuck over and got my ball and hightailed it out of there before they saw me!" Miles said. "I kept that secret too. I can only imagine how much trouble I would have been in if I told on them!" Miles exclaimed. Pa just stood there and didn't say a word.

After the chickens and pigs were fed, Pa and Miles went back up to the house. Time to clean up and go to the hospital. Miles had worn the boots Ma had given him because he knew the sneakers would get real dirty doing the chores on the farm. He laughed at himself as he thought 'working on the farm, who would of thought I would be doing this?' He went inside and changed into his sneakers. Washed his hands, then came back down to the kitchen looking for Ma and Pa. Neither one of them was in the kitchen. He started walking through the house looking for them. He heard voices outside and went towards the front of the house.

Miles opened the front door and saw Officer Bruce standing out there talking to both Ma and Pa. As he stepped out, he saw Ma put her hand on her mouth and started crying. Oh no he thought, was Willy dead? He was afraid to go down and verify that, so he stood on the porch. Pa looked up and called for him to come down.

Pa turned towards Miles as he approached and said "Miles, there has been an incident at the hospital and Officer Bruce was nice enough to stop by and give us an update. It seems Willy woke up early this morning! However, when he did he was screaming and thrashing all over the place." "He is not dead?" Miles asked. "No, but the thrashing he did caused some more damage to his shoulder. Once they got him to calm down, they asked him what was wrong. Willy said 'the last thing he saw was your step-mom holding him down' Pa said.

"I told Officer Bruce we would be going to the hospital in a little while" Pa said. "I am cleaned and ready to go when you are" Miles said. "So Bruce, how is the investigation going? Any news on whether or not they will pay for what they have been doing at that house?" Pa asked.

"I believe we have a good case against them. We have a lot of stuff we are still examining though. Blood samples, finger prints, and various pieces of evidence. We found several new discoveries under the tree and inside the tree. It seems that at least three bodies and one extra skull were found buried there" Officer Bruce explained. "Inside the tree was a box containing what appears to be satanic ritual paraphernalia. Under the house has turned out to be the largest treasure trove though. We found a couple of chests full of household stuff, like silverware sets, polished candlesticks, and a handful of other items" he continued.

"Our most valuable find so far was dug up from under the back of the small shed. It appears that someone was a jewelry thief. High end stuff, like Rolex watches, diamond rings, gold pendants, and bracelets. We found one necklace that the stone alone in it could be worth ten grand" as he finished talking.

"Wow! That is a lot of stuff for a family with only one TV! So, we can assume that someone is going to be in a lot of trouble for all of this?" Pa asked. "Well, we have to figure out who did what first. I find it hard to believe that the mother was the cause of all of these crimes alone. So that leaves us with six children, a father, and the possibility of neighbors and others being involved. We are interviewing each of them to see if anyone will talk. That also means at some point both Miles and Willy will need to be interviewed. Of course, not without you present" Officer Bruce explained.

Miles looked up and said "okay, when you need me, I am ready." "We are also interviewing the neighbors as well. For some reason they seem to know a lot about what has been happening, but never saw the need to say anything before now" Officer Bruce said. "Of course, we will get a child advocate out of the precinct to assist with all of the children. Rebecca has not been cooperative at all. Lewis on the other hand won't stop talking. We had to send Jimmy for a psychiatric evaluation this morning by the

Judge's order. Jimmy's case is going to be sensitive because of his age."

Miles listened to these updates. "Officer Bruce?" Miles asked. "Yes" he responded. "How will all of this work out? Will my stepmother be charged with something because of what she did to Willy? Jimmy, what he did? He was driving the car that ran over Willy. All of my family was arrested and what are you charging them with?" Miles asked. "Well, that is what we are trying to work out. The only two that are actually arrested are Marilyn, your stepmother, and Jimmy, your brother. Your father has been taken to jail and placed into custody for questioning. Carolyn is under the care of Mrs. Johnson, the CPS officer. The children cannot be arrested yet until we find a reason. However, we are able to send them to a Juvenile Detention facility.

"Your stepmother is being charged with accessary to and attempted murder, child endangerment, child abuse, and several charges in connection with the thefts of stolen goods. Your bother, Jimmy, is being charged with attempted murder, using a vehicle as weapon, and driving without a license. Since he is a minor, we have to charge him according to the law for minors. Those are the two main individuals charged so far. As for your father, we are looking at child endangerment, child abuse, and also the thefts of stolen properties. Regarding any charges on Lewis and Rebecca, we have not determined if they were involved or even knew about any of these crimes, other than the abuse going on at your trailer. So far, no body has taken any claim to having stolen the items we have located or the bodies we have found" Officer Bruce continued.

"Do you have enough evidence to convict any of them?" asked Pa. "Yes" Officer Bruce said. "We feel confident that both the mother and father will be convicted on the evidence gathered so far. Jimmy as well. However, we don't want them to get out in a year or so. We need to make sure they pay for what they have done. With the dead bodies and what was done to Willy, the mother is absolutely going to be convicted, even without a confession. We do have a lot of information that we are still combing through. It has only been two days so far and we have a long way to go. I hope by the end of next week to have more definitive answers" Office Bruce finished.

"Let's get ready to go to the hospital Miles" Pa said. "I am ready to go now" he responded. Pa reached out and shook Officer Bruce's hand. Miles and Ma were both standing next to the car ready to load up and head out to the hospital. Pa said "let me run into the house for a moment. Then we can take off."

After Pa took care of what he needed to, he came out and they were standing there hugging each other. Ma turned to Pa and said "Miles is worried about how all of this is happening. He said his biggest worry is that they won't be able to make any of the charges stick. Marilyn will be let free and so will his father. Even if she isn't, the father is just as bad. I am not sure how we can reassure Miles, since we can't even tell him where he ends up."

"Well...as of right this moment, he is staying here. He will continue to stay here until we know enough about how all this will play out. My plan is not to ever send him back to that house. Now I spoke with Bruce again today and one of the things he is going to do is search for Miles' grandparents. If nothing else, they may be an option. But just for today, let's go see Willy and we can work out all the details later."

They loaded up into the car and began to drive to the hospital. As they were heading that way, Pa looked up and told Miles "I told Officer Bruce about your story you told me this morning." "What story is that?" Miles asked. "The story about Lewis and Rebecca" he said. "Oh, okay. That's cool, I just hope it doesn't haunt me later" Miles responded back. Ma looked over confused and wanted to ask, but based on all she knew already, maybe it is best that she not know this story.

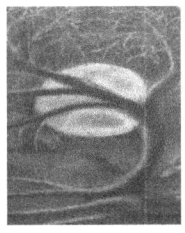

CHAPTER7-A TRUTH REVEALED

They arrived at the hospital and went inside. As they approached Willy's room, Miles began to get nervous. He let Ma go in first, then followed. For some reason Pa stayed in the hallway. Willy was asleep and Ma stepped in next to his bed. Miles walked around to the other side. There were two chairs in the room now, so Ma sat down in one and Miles sat down in the other. They sat there for a short time, not saying anything and Willy began to squirm. Then he opened his eyes. The first thing he saw was his brother. "Hey Miles" he said softly under his breath.

Ma stood up and looked over at Willy. He turned his head and saw a woman he had no idea who she was. He looked over at Miles and gave him a puzzled look. "This is Mrs. Robinson, or Ma as we call her, Willy. She and Pa are letting me stay at their house during all of the stuff going on at home" Miles explained to him. Willy looked over at Miles and started to cry. He said "I am so sorry Miles. I got turned around and didn't go the right way. I couldn't run through the woods because I couldn't see. So I went by the road and she found me. That's when they ran me over."

"It's okay, Willy" Ma said. Willy turned his head and looked at her. "Isn't she your teacher Miles?" he asked. "Yes" Miles said. "How did you end up with her?" Willy asked. "It's a long story, but I will talk to you about it later when we are alone" Miles said. "Would you like me to leave you two alone so you can talk? He seems to be okay, I mean except for the other injuries" Ma stated. "Yeah, but not right now Ma. He needs to get his strength up a little" Miles said.

"The doctor told me this morning that I have two more broken bones. My hip and my shoulder are both broken. They will need to do surgery on me to fix them. He said I am lucky because the ground must have been really soft, allowing my body to sink into the dirt, otherwise I wouldn't be here. Is that true?" Willy asked. "I have not heard about that. Ma did they say anything to you?" Miles asked. "Yes, Officer Bruce did say something to Pa and me. I just did not see the point in passing this information to you. Guess I should have" Ma responded. "It's okay. I probably would have just gotten mad" Miles said.

As they sat there making small talk, Miles could see his friend's spirits getting better. Ma then decided to give them some time alone. After she left, Miles looked over at Willy and told him he wanted him to meet Pa. Miles stood up and walked over to the door and asked Pa if he wanted to come in and meet Willy. "Of course, I have been waiting for this moment" Pa said.

As Pa walked in, Willy looked over at him and his first thought was man this guy is tall! Like the Jolly Green

Giant, only not green! Pa stepped over to his bed and introduced himself. "Hello Willy, my name is James Robinson, but most people just call me Pa." "Hello" Willy said. "So how do you know Miles?" Willy asked Pa. "We found him in our apple orchard two days ago. He is staying at our house until we can get a grip on all that is going on at your house" Pa said.

"Well, good luck with that. You will never find all the rabbit holes at that house" Willy remarked. "I am really sorry about what happened to you. I hope we can help you and Miles get through this and you will be able to heal" Pa said. "The police are doing what they can to investigate everything. Ma and I will do what we can to help you boys and keep you up to date. Just so you know, we filed for guardianship of both of you boys" Pa continued. "Okay. I don't what that means. Just tell Miles, he is the smart one in this family. I probably won't understand what you're talking about" Willy said.

"Well in any case, we want you to know we are here for you. When you get better we will have a room available for you if needed" Pa told Willy. Willy turned and looked at Miles. He went to say something but knew from the look on Miles face to just wait. About that time the doctor came in. "Well...hello Willy. How are you feeling so far today?" Dr. George asked.

"A little sore on this side of my body. It seems to hurt all the way down to here" as he pointed to his hip. "Other than that I am okay. I am glad to see my brother" Willy said. "So Willy, let me explain what is about to happen to you. Since you are awake, we have called for the two specialists to come in and get prepped to do surgery on you, starting with your hip. That surgery will be today, later in the afternoon" Dr. George explained.

"Once your hip surgery is complete, you will rest for twenty four hours, than we will have the second surgery performed. That is if it all goes well after the first one" he continued to explain. Willy looked up and asked the doctor "what exactly is broken on me?" The doctor put up a finger, as if to tell him to hold on and he left the room. A few moments later, he returned with a big chart of the human body. He opened the chart and placed his finger on the hip bone joint. "Right here is a ball joint that holds the hip in place. Your hip's ball is broken off. Up here is the shoulder, which has a similar joint. It is also broken off along with this bone here" Dr. George explained.

"Wow" Willy said! "That sounds really bad! I feel like humpty dumpty" he remarked. "Well, we plan to put you all back together" Dr. George said. "I am glad to see you in such good spirits" Dr. George said. "My brother is here. I am glad to see he is okay" Willy said. "Do you have any questions for me Miles?" Dr. George asked. "When will he be better, so he can leave the hospital?" Miles asked. "Miles, Willy probably won't be able to even get close to leaving the hospital for at least a few weeks. Once his surgeries are completed and we need to confirm his body accepts them okay, then he will have to go through rehabilitation therapy. That's what will determine the length of time. It depends on how fast Willy's body heals" Dr. George explained.

"Okay" Miles said. "Pa, can we come and visit him while he is in here?" Miles asked Pa. "Of course, maybe not every day though. You can talk to him on the phone on the days we can't make it up here" Pa said. "If that is all of your questions, then I need to get back to my other patients. Here in about an hour, we will get Willy ready to do his first surgery. Mr. Mayor, you and Mattie are welcome to stay and visit for as long as you want to" Dr. George said. "What about me?" Miles stepped in and asked. "Sorry Miles, I just assumed you were a given. You weren't planning on going anywhere, were you?" Dr. George responded. "No" said Miles.

Dr. George left and Pa told Miles that he wanted to go out and speak to Ma for a little while. He asked if Miles would watch over Willy while he was gone. Miles just looked at him as if to say, of course. After Pa left, Miles turned around and looked at Willy. "Man...I am so sorry this happened to you!" Miles said. "It's my own fault. You told me which way to go. I got turned around and then I heard Mom tell Jimmy to find me after they had taken all the stuff out of the river" Willy said.

"I heard her say to Jimmy she was going to take me to the pond. She had had enough my shit and it was time for me to go!" Willy said. "I showed them! I'm still here! I know you told me to follow the river. They were down there still, so I took off in the other direction. But it got dark and I couldn't see where I was going, so I went over to the road. I thought if I just stayed close to the woods, I wouldn't be seen" Willy continued to explain what happened.

"The ground was real muddy and I couldn't stay close to the woods. Then suddenly, I heard Jimmy screaming 'yee-haw' and I looked up and saw headlights. Then that was pretty much it. The last thing I saw was Mom putting her foot on me to hold me down, while Jimmy backed the car over me. Goddamn that hurt so bad!" Willy finished. "Dude, it's not your fault! "Miles said. "I went the wrong direction Miles! You told me when the time came to follow the river, so we could come out at the same place, at the Robinsons house!" Willy retorted back.

"Yes, I know" Miles said. "We could not have figured in all the outcomes. I could not have figured out the fact that you were not able to go that direction. Although, I feel bad that you got hurt, I am just glad you made it out and are alive!" Miles said.

"Now listen to me. We need to stick to the plan. Everything else is still in motion. All the stuff is in place to help us get out of this family and have them put away. You need to just be calm and when they ask questions deny everything or play dumb" Miles said. "Okay" Willy said.

"Officer Bruce said they will want to interview us soon and when he does, we can't let them get any ideas that we know how all this happened or that we had anything to do with it! Do you understand? It will be the difference between us going to Juvenile Detention or us going to a new home! Hopefully, Ma and Pa will keep us"

Miles continued. "They like you. I am not on the menu" Willy said. "Well, you actually are. That's why they filed for guardianship on both of us" Miles said. "It gives them the right to make decisions for us and provide us with a home."

"Oh yeah one more thing, I had to improvise this morning. Lewis and Rebecca are having sex now" Miles told Willy. "Man, you are going to hell! All this lying is going to catch up with us!" Willy said. "You know there is no such thing as hell?" Miles said. "You better hope not!" Willy responded. "Just stick to the plan. We will come out better off, I promise" Miles responded back, thinking all of these lies were necessary, so that meant they were good lies and okay to tell.

Pa returned to the room and found them whispering. "What's so private?" he asked. "Oh, it's nothing" Miles said. "We were just telling dirty jokes" he said. "I like dirty jokes" Pa said. "I was telling him about your animals and the place you live in" Miles said. "He was laughing at me being a farmer" Miles continued. Willy turned and looked at Pa. "So, you are the town's Mayor?" Willy asked. "Yes" Pa said. "Cool, I guess. I really don't know what a Mayor is though" Willy said.

"Well, that makes two of us" Pa said. "Miles, Ma and I want to go over to my office and stop in at the police station to talk to Officer Bruce for a little while. Do you think you can stay here with Willy and watch over him? We will be back later today, hopefully before his first surgery?" Pa said. "Yes" Miles said. "Okay" Pa said. "We will see you later. Here is my cell phone. You can call Ma if you need anything. There is no code in it, so you should be able to access her in the contacts list." "Okay" Miles looked at the phone. He had never used one before, so he probably wouldn't need it.

Ma and Pa left leaving Miles and Willy to visit. Miles looked over at Willy and said "they found all this stuff under the house and the jewelry under the shed as well. All that new stuff was just sitting outside the house as well, and one of the officers found the other stuff. This morning they said they found some chests under the house. They found blood stains all over the tree. Also, three bodies were buried around that tree along with a skull. Inside the tree was what Officer Bruce called 'satanic paraphernalia.' They took blood samples from the car they think hit you. Inside the house, they found the tongue in the frame. They took it as well" Miles told Willy.

"As of right now, mom has been arrested, along with Jimmy for what they did to you. Dad has not been arrested yet, but he is being held for questioning. He is looking at child endangerment and child abuse charges. Mom is probably going to go to jail on assisted attempted murder charges, child endangerment, and child abuse. Also, possible charges for theft. Jimmy is being charged with attempted murder because he was driving. However, he is a minor according to Officer Bruce and they did a psych evaluation on him" as Miles continues to update Willy.

"What is a psych evaluation?" Willy asked Miles. "It's when they check to see if you are crazy" Miles said. "Well, we already know he qualifies for that!" Willy said.

"So far everything is working out how we planned it. If we keep our cool and let them do their investigation, you and I should be home free. Rebecca and Lewis will go to Juvenile Detention. Carolyn will be sent to CPS to a foster home eventually. I hope Dad, Mom, and Jimmy are put in jail and you and I will end up at the Robinson's house" Miles said.

"You don't think at any point in this someone is going to spill the beans on us? I mean, after all you recruited the neighbors as well. When those bodies were removed from the pond, you had the Rogers boys help us. As for all the stuff under the house, I didn't know if you did that. What jewelry was left behind the shed?" Willy asked Miles. "I paid them really well to help us out. Good thing Mom doesn't check her safe very often. She didn't miss the gold bars I took to pay them with. As for the stuff under the house, that wasn't me. I have no idea how that stuff got there" Miles said.

"The jewelry under the shed was one of my little inputs. I think it is best that you not know how I pulled that one off. Okay?" Miles asked. "Okay" Willy responded. Miles just grinned as if he was proud of himself. All of the planning they did over the past year and a halfway now playing out, and he was just watching their plans unfold. So far, outside of Willy getting hit by the car, everything has gone well. His only hope is that he hid any evidence of his and Willy's involvement from the police good enough.

However, Miles was worrying about whether or not his calculations of Mrs. Robinson's response was correct. So far, he was right on target. Although, he was unable to factor in the guardianship decision. That was quite a surprise. Mrs. Robinson is one of the few people that actually treated him like she was interested in him and cared. She could see his intelligence and didn't get upset when he was ahead of everyone else in her class. He felt like she took it as a compliment to her teaching abilities. She was a good person all around, and the one thing he hoped for was that she believed in his and Willy's innocence. All of the things him and Willy have done and the lies that they were telling, had been to get people's attention to the terrible things that were happening in their house and to allow him and Willy to escape.

The nurse came in and announced that it was time to prepare Willy for his first surgery. Miles stood up and asked where he needed to go. The nurse said he could stay in the room or go out to the waiting room back in the hall. She said there were vending machines there if you were hungry. "It's okay" he said. "I don't have any money and I am okay." The nurse turned towards Willy and began giving him a sedative in his intravenous tube. Then she checked his vital signs in preparation for his surgery. Miles headed down the hall to the waiting area.

A short time later, he saw Willy and his bed being pushed down the hall to surgery. Now all he needed to do is wait. Miles looked around and found out that they had a whole rack of magazines that he could read. He fumbled through them and found one that he might like, Motorsport with newer cars. Cool, Miles thought. He sat down and began to read.

After a while, he heard a voice say 'wake up boy.' It was Pa standing over him. He and Ma had returned from their trip, while Miles had fallen asleep. "Is Willy in surgery?" Ma asked. "Yes" Miles said. "He was when I sat down. I don't know how long I have been here. I must have fallen asleep." "I will ask the nurse how it is going" Ma said. Pa sat down next to Miles and stared at him. "Miles, it appears there is a lot of information the police are gathering and Officer Bruce would like to speak to you again today" Pa said.

"I told him he could come see you here or at the house later. I believe he will be coming here this afternoon" Pa finished. "Okay. Have they found out anything new?" Miles asked. "Yes, there is quite a bit of new information. I think we will let him talk to you first and then we will talk later" Pa said. "Sounds like I am in trouble" Miles looked worried. "Should you be Miles? Is there something you would want to say now to maybe not be in trouble for later?" Pa asked. This is a trick question Miles thought. "No, nothing that I know of" he said.

Pa had sat down and they waited for Ma to return. A lady walked over and said she needed to talk to Pa. Pa stood up and followed her into her office. A short while later, Pa came back out and asked Miles to follow him. They both walked over to the office with a door that said Accounting on it. As Miles stepped in, she looked up at Pa. "He is a child" she said. "Yes" Pa said. "He may be able to help you with your questions. Let's just ask him, so we can find out what is going on" Pa said. "Miles, we are having trouble finding your family and your brother's name in any of our networks. What is Willy's last name?" the office lady asked.

"Travois, his name is Willy Travois" Miles said. "Okay, well...let us see what that does. Is that the mother's last name as well?" she asked. "Yes" Miles responded. "Well there she is but I'm still not finding him. Let me do some research and see if we have any records on him. Thank you Miles for your help" she said. "Your welcome" Miles said. Pa turned and asked her if there was anything else she needed. "Well, I have to find him because we are trying to do a Medicaid claim and we need him to show up as a person. Otherwise, someone is going to have to cough up a lot of money to pay for all of his medical bills" she responded.

"How much money?" Miles asked. She looked over at Pa and he gave her the sign to go ahead. "Well, as of today we have a balance of $88,065.00. That doesn't include today's surgery or the next one. Also, all of the rehabilitation that needs to be done. I wouldn't worry too much Miles; it's mostly a matter of us finding his name in the system so we can file a claim. If not, we will need to do some research to find what hospital he was born at and get a birth certificate. Your mother or father, neither one, were carrying any medical insurance from what we can tell" she explained.

"I don't know if they have any medical insurance or not. I have never been to the hospital before. When we went to the doctor the last time, my mother paid with cash" Miles said. "When was that?" she asked. "Lewis broke his arm falling out of a tree last year. We went to some house and it took a few hours to get there. I don't remember it having a doctor's sign on it, but it must have. They fixed his arm. Cost her about one hundred dollars" Miles explained. "Do you remember what town you went to?" she asked. "No" Miles said. "It was way out in the country. An old man and woman was there. They had a whole bunch of kids running around" Miles said.

"Okay, we will keep looking from here. Hopefully something will come up" she responded. Miles and Pa went back to the waiting room. "Pa, if you take me over to the house, we can get some cash to pay the bill. Mom has a stash she keeps hidden in the back bedroom. I am sure there will be enough" Miles said. "I beg your pardon?" Pa said. "She doesn't know we know about it. But she is not real smart and her security is not very good" Miles said. "How much money are you talking about?" Pa asked.

"I don't know, but I am sure there is enough to pay this bill. She keeps one hundred dollar bills in her hidden spot. She has stacks of them. If that's not enough, she has a pile of gold bars" Miles said. "Gold bars! I assume you know where she keeps them?" Pa asked. "Of course, we all do. We know not to mess with it because she would kill us if we did" Miles said. "Where did all this money come from?" Pa asked.

"Rebecca said it comes from the family business. She said it will all be hers one day when Mom dies. When someone in the family needs something taken care of or disposed of they call Mom. She said mom has been teaching her to run the business" Miles said. "Where does her family live?" Pa asked. "All over the place. Some live close by us and some live all across the country. A couple live in Oklahoma, but most of them live here in Texas" Miles responded.

Pa looked at Miles somewhat confused, "Miles, where do you think Little Elm is located?" Pa asked. "Texas, it is real close to my Grandpa and Grandma's home. They live in Grand View, Texas" Miles said. "Miles, Little Elm is not located in Texas or Oklahoma. We are in New Mexico, and I am not aware of a town named Grand View anywhere near here" Pa said. "New Mexico? No, that can't be right because there is a Texas sign outside of our trailer park" Miles said.

"A sign? You can show that to me next time we go out there. Which after I call Bruce, maybe here in a little while; I am not sure what time he was planning on coming to speak to you anyway" Pa said to Miles. How is this possible? He seems so smart, but has no idea which state he is in currently Pa thought.

Pa got up and walked over to Ma. She was sitting over by the nurse's station. He told her what Miles and he had been talking about. She turned and looked at Pa "oh...it can't be possible that he thinks he is in Texas. He knows all the states by heart. Let me talk to him" Ma said.

Ma and Pa walk over and sit down next to Miles. "Miles, honey" Ma said. He looked over and he knew what she is about to say. "I don't know Ma" Miles said. "I do not know how I could have gotten this so wrong. All this time I thought they moved us to a new town in Texas. I just remember when we came here, I fell asleep. I woke up here at the trailer park. The only time we ever left the trailer park was when we went to one of her families houses out in the country or we went to school. When we go to her family, it is so far I usually fall sleep. I am thinking about how I could have missed that I am two states over!" Miles said.

Ma looked over at Pa, than turned back to Miles. "Why did you sleep?" Ma asked. "Before we leave on a trip, she makes us drink some stuff she mixes up. It doesn't taste too bad but it makes me really tired" Miles said. "Is your father in the car?" Pa asked. "Yes, He drives. It is one of the only times he is not drunk and falling all over himself" Miles said. "Does everyone go?" Ma asked. "Yes" Miles said. "All of us."

Pa gets up and looks at Ma. Ma stands and tells Miles she and Pa want to talk and need to be excused. As they walk away, Miles sat there and thinking about how he could have not known he wasn't in the state of Texas anymore. All this time he had planned out everything, it never occurred to him to check his location. He never thought to look up Little Elm before because when they went to his grandparents it was so close. Of course he did sleep the whole way. He wondered what was in that drink.

Pa came back over and told Miles he had called Officer Bruce who was coming to pick them up at the hospital. They were going to go back to the house to meet some officers there. "He wants you to show him the money and gold bars stashes, then he will talk with you some more. There have been many developments in the case and he has a lot of questions that are not adding up" Pa told Miles. Miles was not sure what that meant, but he looked back and nodded his head anyway.

Ma stood up as a doctor came out of surgery. "Is he okay?" Ma asked. "Better than okay Mrs. Robinson. He came through his surgery with flying colors. No problems with his breathing and the operation went really well. We were lucky he had no other damage at his hip. It will take a few days before he can get up and start moving around. Then once that starts, he can start rehabilitation" Dr. Edwards said. "By the way, my name is Dr. Edwards" he introduced himself to Ma.

"Well, it's good to meet you Dr. Edwards. My name is Mattie Robinson. I am so glad to hear this. A few days...that's really good to hear! I had figured that it would take at least a week or so before he stood up" Ma said. "Oh no, with today's technology, we don't want him to get comfortable. The faster we get him up, the faster we help him heal" the doctor replied. "I understand he will be having another surgery in a few days, possibly tomorrow. We will work with the next surgeon to make sure we collaborate on all that is involved" Dr. Edwards told Ma.

"Okay. I am just excited everything is going so well for Willy!" Ma said. She turned around and found Pa and Miles were standing directly behind her. So she didn't see any reason to give an update to them. Pa looked at Ma and said "Officer Bruce is on his way over to pick Miles and me up. We will be leaving for a little while to go back to Miles' house. Here are the keys to our car if you need to leave here." "Okay. Please let me know what you find out" Ma said.

"Will do" Pa responded. Miles knew that he was starting to look a little suspicious. He thought if there was anything he could say that would make them believe him he was going to say it. "I am sorry you are having to deal with all of our stuff" he said. "I wish we didn't have to do all of this." Ma looked up and she smiled, reached out her arms and gave him a hug. "You boys are just too young to have to know this much about the world. You should be playing in some field somewhere kicking a ball or something. Not trying to survive because you are afraid of being hurt or even killed. I only want you to see that we care about you, but we need you to be honest with us" Ma said. "Yes ma'am" Miles said.

Pa and Miles went to the front door of the hospital to wait for Officer Bruce to pick them up. As they waited, Pa turned to Miles and looked straight at him. "Miles" he said. "Ma said that when Willy woke up the first thing he said was he was sorry he went the wrong way. He was supposed to go back the way you did. Do you know why he said that?" Oh man Miles thought. He looked up at Pa and admitted "yes. For years now we have talked about leaving there. We planned that if one of us had to go first, then the other would follow them in the same direction. I spoke to Willy when you were out of the room. He got turned around because Mom, Lewis, Rebecca, and Jimmy were all down in the river where I took off at" Miles told Pa.

"He heard her say to Jimmy that when they were done getting all the stuff from the river, he needed to get Willy and they were going to the pond. So Willy got spooked and took off the wrong way. That's how he got caught" Miles finished. "Do I want to know what the pond means?" Pa asked. "It's where we go to die. I have only been there once, but Rebecca said that she and her mom have taken other kids down there. Mom ties a brick to their legs heavy enough to weigh them down. Then she pushes them into the water and watches them drown" Miles said.

Pa looked at Miles and his first thought was oh my God! "Why didn't you say anything to me or Officer Bruce about this?" "I don't know. We don't talk about stuff at our house, so I guess I forgot until now. Mom owns all the property way back into and past the woods. The pond is way back deep in there. I have only been there once with Willy" Miles said. "That is a big forget!" Pa said.

"How many children are supposedly in that pond Miles?" Pa asked. "I don't know" he responded. "Rebecca is not the best source of information. She is a lot like Mom and lies a lot. You can't trust anything she says. So if you talk to her, she isn't going to be much help. She told me that all of us kids were from other homes. She said that we were brought to Mom to dispose of because no one else wanted us. When Mom gets tired of a kid, she just gets rid of them. Sometimes, she sells them but the rest are put in the pond" Miles said to Pa.

"I don't really know what to believe that Rebecca tells me all the time. I know for fact that me, Lewis, Jimmy, and Carolyn were all together before we came here. As well as my Dad. So, we aren't from other homes separately nor do we belong to anyone else" Miles said. About that time Officer Bruce arrived. They both climbed into his vehicle and he started driving towards the trailer park. "Pa said you have some things you want to talk to me about?" Miles asked Officer Bruce. "Yes" he said. "I have been talking to your brother and Rebecca and your version of the truth doesn't line up with theirs. Also, your neighbors are not being very helpful to your story either" Officer Bruce said.

Pa turned to Officer Bruce and said "have you heard about the pond?" "It has been mentioned a time or two" he responded. "Well, we heard about it this morning. Along with the fact that there is a stash of money and gold on the property, which is why I called you" Pa said. Officer Bruce looked over at Pa and then turned back to Miles. "Okay here is the deal. I need the honest version of what is going on. If I cannot get good information, then what is going to happen is Willy and you are going to be investigated for a lot of evidence tampering, theft, and a host of other items that seem to involve a handful of scheming. Although we have a good case against your mother and Jimmy, we cannot find enough evidence that will allow us to charge your father or Rebecca."

"Because your neighbors are telling me you and Willy have been sneaking out at night and using one of the older lady's trucks to steal all that stuff we found at the river. Lewis and Rebecca both deny any sort of sexual relationship, which truthfully has no bearing on anything."

"I was even told that you paid two of the neighbor boys to move bodies from the pond and bury them by the tree. Miles, I cannot do my job without the truth and if I find out you and Willy are involved in any of these crimes, there will be trouble for the both of you! Do you understand?" Officer Bruce sternly asked Miles. "Yes sir. Do you want the whole story or just the easy version?" Miles asked. "All of it! Give me the whole damn story!" Officer Bruce said.

"When we moved here, Willy and I hit it off right away. My step-mother seemed to be always looking for some reason to punish us, so we would sneak away from the house and go somewhere to play and hide. One day we were way back in the woods when we walked up to this pond of water. It had a peer on the edge of it. So I said, hey let's go back and get some fishing poles and see if there are fish in the pond. Willy stopped and wouldn't go another step. He looked like he had seen a ghost. I was like, what's wrong dude?" as Miles began to tell the unvarnished true story.

"Willy stood there frozen and said "that's the pond. We can't go near there." I was like 'why not?' 'That's where the kids are' he said to me. 'What kids?' I asked. He turned to me and said that 'all of these kids are brought to our house because no one wants them. So they give them to Mom to get rid of. Some she sells to other people, but if they make it to twelve years old, she brings them here. She ties one of those bricks to their legs and pushes them into the water and watches them drown' Miles continued his story.

"At first I thought he was joking, but he was actually turning white. He was scared to death of that pond. I told him 'oh bull' and I walked over to the pond and looked over the side and that's when I realized he wasn't joking. The water was real clear and I could see a hand attached to an arm, swaying under water. I took off running and Willy came after me" Miles continued.

"It took me a while to calm down that day. Then I remembered that when we moved to this house, there was another boy living there. He was about twelve years old. His name was Tim. One day he was gone. I asked and was told to mind my own business by Rebecca. She said that 'if I ask too many questions, I will find out the hard way where he went.' For a while Willy and I quit hanging out, then one day I started talking to him again" as Miles continued his story.

'Why won't you talk to me Willy?' I asked him. He said that he 'didn't want to talk about what we saw.' Well I said to him 'technically you didn't see anything, I did.' Willy said he 'doesn't want to end up in there.' I said 'well, when you and I turn twelve, if we are still here, we are both going to end up in that pond. We need to do something now'" he continued.

"You were eight years old then?" Officer Bruce said. "Well almost nine" Miles said. "Still you were so young. How does a young boy understand all of this?" Pa chimed in. "Self-preservation" Miles said. "After I saw that arm, I knew we had to do something. I wanted to call the cops, but Willy said they had been out to that house many times and never seemed to look around. All of the neighbors have called the police for different for reasons too, hoping something will happen. So I began to come up with a plan to hopefully stop what has been going on for a long time" Miles finished.

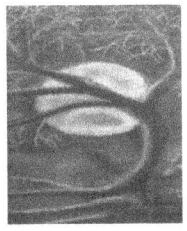

CHAPTER 8- DIRTY LITTLE SECRETS

Officer Bruce looked over at Pa. "You wanted to know how much worse this could get?" he said. "Huh" Pa huffed. "There is one flaw in your story" Office Bruce said to Miles. "What is that?" Miles asked. "Lewis is fourteen years old and Jimmy is twelve. If your story is correct, then neither of them would still be here" Officer Bruce exclaimed. "Well, Lewis belongs to Rebecca. He is her little toy and I don't know why Jimmy is still alive" Miles said. "What?" Pa asked. "When we moved here, Lewis was twelve years old and so was Rebecca. Rebecca told Mom she wanted to keep him. She wanted to practice the family business on him. So Mom gave her Lewis. They took him down to the pond and showed him his future if he didn't do as he was told" Miles explained.

"So did you actually see them having sex?" Officer Bruce asked. "No" said Miles. "I made that up, but I know they slept together in the house and I have seen them naked before. So although the barn story wasn't exactly true, I believe they were having sex" Miles responded. "Well, they are denying it very convincingly" Officer Bruce said. "I can show you the bed they sleep in. You can investigate it if you like" Miles said. "I had a forensics group go through there earlier, but we can check it again today" Officer Bruce said.

Officer Bruce was giving Pa a look of disbelief. However, he picked up his phone and called the police station to tell the lead officer on duty that he needed a forensic team sent back out to the Dingwald house again. Just then Officer Bruce drove around the corner, entering the trailer park.

That's when Miles shouted "there!" pointing to a sign on the street. Both Pa and Officer Bruce looked up to see a sign that said 'Texas City 10 miles.' Pa looked back at Miles and said "Miles, that sign is letting you know how far it is to the next town that is called Texas City. It just happens to have Texas in its name." "Oh" he responded. Every now and then this boy does something that reminds everyone of how young he really is Pa thought.

They pulled up to the house and noticed that the front door was open. As they parked, out came Mr. Bufford, the neighbor. Officer Bruce stopped the vehicle and got out. "What in the world are you doing in this house Mr. Bufford?" "Um...um...um looking around" he finally said. "For what?" Officer Bruce scolded him. "There is absolutely no reason for you to be in that house unless you are stealing something! In that case, we are going to arrest you right now for breaking and entering!"

"No reason to get huffy, Officer. I was just nosing around. Rumor has it she has been keeping a gold mine in this house. Just thought I would see for myself" Mr. Bufford said. "Did you find what you were looking for?" Miles asked. "Nope" he said as he turned to go back to his home. "Moron" Miles said under his breath just loud enough for Pa to hear him. As Miles climbed out of the vehicle, Pa followed. "So what do you want to see first the pond or the money?" Miles asked. "The money and gold!" Pa and Officer Bruce said at the same time.

Miles walked towards the trailer's front door and noticed the door lock had been broken. He pointed to it as they walked in. "Look at this! Someone has broken the lock" Miles said. "Do you think Mr. Bufford may be the culprit?" Pa asked. "No" said Miles. "He may be nosy, but he is a nice guy and I wouldn't think he would try to rob us" Miles responded. They followed Miles back through the house towards the very back room of the house. All through the house, clothes and personal items are thrown about everywhere. Miles turned and looked back at both Pa and Officer Bruce. "It wasn't like this the other day. Guess the police aren't watching over this place very well" Miles said.

"Well in our defense Miles, we are only getting information in bits and pieces. How are we supposed to know all your neighbors were going to try and rob this house and steal its treasure? We had no idea a treasure existed!" Officer Bruce responded. "Had we been given good information, we might have done a better job" he continued. "Good point" Pa said. "Yeah, I guess you are right. No more lies" Miles returned. As they shuffled their way to the back room, Miles stopped and pointed to the next to the last room "Lewis and Rebecca sleep here" he said.

They entered the back room of the house, and Miles just laughed. "Morons" he said talking about the robbers. He opened the closet and asked both Officer Bruce and Pa "which one do you want to see first? The gold or the cash? The one is on the left or the other on the right?" Miles explained. Officer Bruce said "either one."

Miles reached up and pulled the clothes on the left side of the hangers and pushed them all the way to the right. Then he reached back and moved the shoes out of the way. Then taking his fingers, he pressed them into the side up against the corner, allowing him to slide the back wall over to the right, all the way until it opened. Inside there was a metal box about four feet tall and three feet wide. Miles reached over and opened the door of the box. He stepped back and let the Officer and Pa see the contents.

One hundred dollar bills were stacked inside vacuum packed plastic wraps. The stacks filled in half of the box. Miles sat back and let both of them take in the sight with a smirk on his face. Officer Bruce looked up and asked the question "where did all this money come from? Why are you living in this trailer if you have all this money?" "Well, as for where it came from, I don't know. I just knew she had it because Willy had told me about it a long time ago. We live here I think because no one will care about us if we look poor" Miles said.

"Officer Bruce, can we take this money and use it to pay Willy's bill at the hospital?" Miles asked. "Um…um…well I don't know Miles. We need to determine how all of this money came about" Officer Bruce answered. "Are you ready for the best part?" Miles asked. They step back and Miles shuts the door on the box. He reaches over and pulled the back piece over to the left and placed it back into position. He then moved the shoes and clothes back to the left. Then he moved the clothes on the right over to the left. He pushed his fingers into the corner and slid the back wall over to the left. Again, exposing another box the same size.

This box had a small latch with a small lock on it. He pushed the lock, clicking it, and then unlatched the box and opened its door. Behind him Miles heard both men make a moaning noise. Before them were stacks of gold bars. Pa said "there must be a hundred gold bars in there! Take one out and see how big each one is!" "Five troy ounces each! Sorry, I had to borrow some a while back, so I found out then" Miles said. "You had to borrow some" Officer Bruce looked over at Miles questioning him.

"Yes, I borrowed some. It turns out our neighbors don't do stuff for free" Miles explained. "Mom counted her cash stacks all the time. She very seldom opened this box. I needed some money to get help, so I took a couple of the bars. I placed this cardboard under the lower stacks, so she wouldn't know any were missing." "Help for what?" Pa asked. "Well, that was part of my plans to set her and my Dad up for all the stuff they had done to us. Willy and me are too small to move some of the things to the riverbed that we needed to move, so I recruited some help" Miles said. "We would not have had to go through all of this if had you and the rest of the police force had done their jobs in the first place! The two officers that came out that she paid off were another issue!" Miles said.

"Excuse me?" Officer Bruce said. "She gave two of your officers each, one of the stacks of one hundred dollar bills. That was one thousand dollars each" Miles said. "Officer Ramirez and Officer Carl came out last year and looked around. She gave them that money to get them turn their backs and walk away" Miles said. "We never saw them again after that. It has always been someone else." "Those are really serious charges son. I have been with this force for fifteen years and I don't know of any officers by those names" Officer Bruce said.

Miles looked at both men and asked if he could close up the box. They both stepped back to allow him access, so he could put things back to the original place. Afterwards they discussed what was next. "Well...we have to wait until the forensic team gets here. Now that we know your neighbors are willing to rob you blind, we need to guard this house. At least until we get all of this money and gold out of here. Let me make some more calls and I will work on getting this handled. Then we are going to go to the pond" Officer Bruce said.

Officer Bruce stepped over to his vehicle and made a few phone calls. Once he was done, he rejoined Pa and Miles who were talking. "I know what I did was probably wrong but I didn't want to die. I should have called the police and told them everything. But do you think I would have had any better luck had I not gone through you?" Miles asked to Pa. "So let me see if I am understanding what I have learned over the last few days. You planned all of this, including you showing up at my house? Am I correct?" Pa asked. "Most of it. Yes. I attend school in Ma's class and I found out where she lived. When I figured out it was really close to us, I worked it out so we could come to you hoping I would get the help we needed. I didn't know you were the town Mayor" Miles said.

"I am sorry for lying to you both. I just needed someone to help and it turns out you just lived the closest" Miles responded to Pa's remarks. "Well" Pa said, "I am somewhat bummed by this thought and at the same time amazed!" "Okay" Officer Bruce stepped in at this point. "So that you will know, I just got off the phone with our lab and it turns out the DNA we have pulled on all of these kids except one doesn't match anyone at that house" he told Pa and Miles.

"How is that possible?" Pa asked. "I don't know Pa" Officer Bruce said. "All I do know is everything we do on this case reveals a new mystery. Right now I am having them check all the DNA samples against both the police database and medical databases" he continued. As they were talking, a van and a police car arrived and pulled up to the house. The van had the forensic group in it and the two officers had their own police car. Officer Bruce instructed the forensic team to have one or two of their team check the room Miles designated as Rebecca and Lewis's room for any signs of sexual activity. The two officers were instructed to guard the house.

The rest of the team went with them to the pond location. "How do we get to this pond?" Officer Bruce asked Miles. "It is way over there in the woods, on the other side" Miles said. "Can we drive over there?" Officer Bruce asked. "I don't know, we never did" Miles said. "When Willy and I went there, we walked to it" Miles said. "Okay, then we walk. You can lead the way" Officer Bruce told Miles. "Yes sir" he said.

The forensic team gathered their tools and equipment and followed Miles as he set out across the field toward the wooded area. As they approached, Officer Bruce could see the tree that Miles and Willy had been beaten at. He stopped and walked over to the location. The team stopped, thinking Officer Bruce wanted them to wait for him. He waved the lead officer on over the hill and down into the river base. A trail that had been walked many times was easy to cross. Getting back up the hill was a different story. The trail was easy to see, but the hill was really steep and the weeds and vines in it had grown across some areas. "It doesn't look like anyone has been on this side for some time" Pa said to Miles.

"Yeah, we haven't come this way other than the one time I told you about. Well that's not exactly true as you will eventually learn" Miles responded. "It's not a place I want to visit for sure" he continued. "Are you guys going to make it?" Pa asked the forensic team. "Oh yeah, not our first climb" said the lead tech. As they crossed over the hill, Miles pointed out that the trail goes in two directions. "We want to go left. I hope Officer Bruce figures that out" Miles said. "I got it" Officer Bruce said as he snuck back into the group.

"Find anything new at the tree?" Pa asked. "No" Officer Bruce responded. "Just wanted to see for myself what I have been told" he said. "This is so surreal that I am having to ground myself to make sure it is real. I didn't just fall asleep and it was all a dream" Officer Bruce told Pa. "Well if this is a dream to you, I would really hate to see your nightmares!" Pa said. The trail was really clear and surrounding them was a forest of trees. Many of which are full of new leaves. Winter has passed and all of the foliage was turning green since it was Spring.

Down the trail, two trees had fallen over onto the trail but were not on the ground. The team could walk under them. "That's interesting" Pa said. "Yeah, the trees fell over during the last freeze we had" Miles said. "A lot of the trees in the forest lost limbs. Over in that area is a big pile of limbs that broke off the trees. We found a dead deer that had been stabbed when a limb fell on him" Miles said. "That was a big feast!" he remarked. "Here we are" Miles said as he pointed out past the tree line. "Right there is the pond. It has a peer that goes out half way. You will notice the blocks on the peer" Miles pointed out. As they approached, Officer Bruce saw someone out of the corner of his eyes.

Covering the area was a bunch of grass that has grown three feet in height. The tree line had stopped and it was an open field. The trail in front of them was partially covered but still noticeable. As they walked along the trail, grasshoppers and other insects jumped across the trail. It was serenely quiet in the field.

"Stop!" Officer Bruce said. "There is something over there to the right. I think it is a person. Hey you over there, come out and show yourself!" he hollered. Nothing happened and no one moved. He hollered again "I can see you, I am with the Little Elm Police and you need to show yourself." Again nothing. Officer Bruce pulled out his service weapon and announced "I have a gun and I will use it! Now, you need to show yourself or I will start shooting! Put your hands above your head and come out!" A set of hands raised up over the weeds and a person stood up. "Don't shoot" he said. Miles recognized that voice.

It was Lewis. How did he get out of Juvenile Detention? Officer Bruce walked over and placed hand cuffs on Lewis. "What are you doing here?" Miles blurted out at Lewis. "You are supposed to be in Juvenile Detention!" he continued. Lewis looked like he was scared out of his mind. He was shaking and started to cry. "I snuck out last night. Rebecca told me to come here and clean out the pond. She told me to take them to the cooker and burn the bodies so no one could find them. She can't know that you are here or I will be toast!" Lewis said. "Your secret is safe with us" said Officer Bruce. "I was told there were six, but I can only find three" Lewis responded. Miles looked up and said "well that's because the other three have been moved."

Officer Bruce looked up and said "Moved to where, Miles?" "We buried them under the tree. I haven't told you this part of the story" Miles said. Officer Bruce looked back at Lewis. "Where are the bodies you found?" Lewis pointed back towards the area where Officer Bruce saw him. Officer Bruce looked up and called the lead forensic tech over. "Let's surround the pond and start looking for evidence. Anything you can find that might place the suspects here or indicate who was involved in all of this. Also, we need to get these bodies back to the lab, so please call for a bus to come out. Let's hope no evidence was destroyed due to these bodies being moved. I can hear a road over there, so we might be able to access this area from there. Miles, do you know about this cooker?" Officer Bruce asked. "News to me" Miles said.

"Lewis, please lead the way" Officer Bruce instructed him. Lewis turned and started walking in the direction away from the pond. The forensic group stayed behind except for one of the team. That person came with Lewis, Pa, Miles, and Officer Bruce. This time there were no trails. The walk was challenging. "Are you sure about this Lewis?" Officer Bruce asked him. "Yes sir, I am sure. Mom wanted to keep this area private. She only used it for special occasions" Lewis said. Lewis walked them back into the woods, where they had to cut out some briar bushes to get around the hill that led them to the site. It was well hidden and very remote.

"It is right over there" Lewis pointed. Standing about twenty feet in front of them was the most bizarre sight any of them had ever seen. A temple of sorts. Built from blocks of rocks that were moved here from the riverbed. Big stones were stacked and placed to form some kind of demon or a cow statue Miles thought. At the bottom was a big hole and a fire pit. A rod was hanging inside the pit from side to side. The remanence of burned bones and flesh were still present.

Officer Bruce noticed what looked like a mantle and on the top of it was a small box. Officer Bruce pointed to the box, put on a pair of gloves, and reached over to pick up the box. He opened it and found it was full of a stack of pictures. At least twenty of them. He picked up the pictures and began looking through them. There were photographs of children, adults, women, men, girls, and boys. All looking as if they had been beaten severely and then placed up there to show off their injuries or as a trophy image for someone to look at.

"Wow, this is not what I expected to find! Let me guess, these people were sacrifices?" Officer Bruce looks over at Lewis. "Yes sir" Lewis said. "She would pick whoever she wanted, brought them up here, and performed her ritual. I have only been here one time and watched her ritual. The last time she let Rebecca perform it" Lewis continued. "After watching her ritual, the pond didn't look so bad" Lewis remarked. "How does she pick who to sacrifice?" Miles asked. "I don't know. The last one was a little boy named Tim. That was the one Rebecca did" Lewis said. "I think the person before that was one of Mom's husbands" he continued. As they stared at the temple, Officer Bruce turned to the forensic tech and pointed to the pit. "Let's get started gathering evidence so we can get out of here before nightfall" he said.

Miles looked up and saw that Pa was sitting on a log about twenty or so feet away from the site. Miles walked over and sat down next to him. Pa looked down at this young boy, Miles, and just sat there. Miles didn't say a word. "I cannot possibly understand what you have gone through. I am so sorry we never saw this at all. I hate that you children have all been subjected to some of the worse abuse and terrorizing fear possible!" Pa said to Miles.

Officer Bruce looked over at them and then went back to work. He moved Lewis over to the side and told him to sit down, he would deal with him later. "Are you going to arrest me?" Lewis asked. "I don't know yet, but we can't take you back to Juvie where Rebecca can have access to you and hurt you anymore. I have to get her into custody" Officer Bruce told him.

Miles watched as Officer Bruce and the tech was going through the pit, taking pictures of the temple and everything. They were looking for finger prints and anything that could identify who was doing these rituals and used this site. Miles thought to himself 'you did it. You finally did it! You won!' he thought. Then he thought back to what had happened up to this point. Willy was almost killed. Lewis was being sacrificed to Rebecca. So many terrible things going on right in front of peoples noses including his.

"Okay" Officer Bruce announced. "I have one more question for Lewis. Do you know where the camera that was used to take these pictures is?" Lewis answered "over there under those stones." The tech turned around and walked over and looked under the stones. She pulled out the camera and a couple of metal objects. "What are these?" she asked Lewis. "They used those to torture them before they cooked them" Lewis said. "Why do they cook these people?" Officer Bruce asked. "It is a sacrifice to the God she serves. She said a bad person must be sacrificed to bring her riches" Lewis explained.

"Let's get going back to the pond and see what they may have found. We also need to get the money out of that house. The banker should be there by now. Grace, do you think we will need to come back tomorrow for more work?" Officer Bruce asked the forensic tech. "Let me get back and talk to Gene and see if he believes we need more time to gather evidence. I think we may have enough now to make some charges stick" Grace said. "Hopefully, we will be able to get either some DNA or finger prints on some of this evidence" Grace said. She gathered up her evidence, tools, and equipment and loaded them into her sack to carry back to the van. All the evidence was bagged and tagged for when it would be sent to the lab for processing. They all started heading back towards the pond to get an update.

Walking back through the woods to the pond, Officer Bruce stopped and spoke with Gene, the lead tech. He asked if any evidence had been found that could help their case. Gene said they had found several cigarette butts in the area by the peer. They found a tie and a shirt with blood on it. He wanted to have some divers come in and swim under water to see if anything had been missed. He knew there had to be some sort of weight at the bottom of the pond to hold any more bodies down. Other than that, the three additional bodies have been sent back to the lab for autopsy, as well as most of the evidence. Officer Bruce was happy that they were able to find more evidence. He said to Gene "we need to get everything we have gathered together and get back to the trailer. I have a banker waiting there for me to deal with another issue. So go ahead and get your people together and let's go to the trailer."

Gene looked up and over at his team. They were still walking through the fields and it looked like they needed more time. "If you don't mind sir, we really would like to continue our search. Even though we feel as if we may have enough evidence with the bodies and other items collected, we want to verify that there is no other evidence out here that will help point to both of the current suspects. As of right now, all of the evidence may still not be enough to convict the suspects. And we need to build verifiable evidence that will nail these people. "

"What do you think about us bringing in divers?" Gene asked Officer Bruce. "Do you think there are more bodies to be discovered?" Officer Bruce asked. "Well, the evidence we have so far supports that possibility. Over here on the peer, we found signs that something may be in the water at this point. Our sonar picked it up, but we cannot see anything visually. I feel like we need to take a closer look" Gene said. "Sounds good to me. You want to do that part tomorrow and finish what you are doing here tonight?" Officer Bruce asked him. "Yes" He answered.

Office Bruce dialed his phone to the station and asked for Officer Green. "Officer Bruce how can I help you?" Officer Green said. "I need you to send an officer over to the Juvenile Detention center and arrest Rebecca Travois under murder charges, assisted murder…the same charges that the mother has been arrested on. Also, can you find a different detention center that we can put Lewis Dingwald in? I appreciate your assistance with this. We will go over all the information later today. Hopefully, the lab will have some answers by this afternoon" Officer Bruce said.

Officer Bruce looked over at Pa and Miles standing there waiting for him with the other officers, waiting to go back to the trailer. He walked over and just stood there. No one was talking now. Once everyone was ready that was going back to the trailer, they began walking back down the trail they had come down on. Miles finally spoke up "Holy cow, never did I see any of this coming at all! I have lived here for two years and had no idea about some of this!" Pa looked up and just nodded his head. Officer Bruce looked over at Miles and said "and you still haven't told me the rest of your story." Miles responded "after all of this, you still need me to do that?" "Understanding your part in all of this will hopefully provide us with enough motive to prevent an issue with all the tampering you, Willy, and now Lewis have done" Officer Bruce explained.

"We also have dug up evidence that made us believe that your stepmother's whole family is deeply embedded some sort of criminal activity. We don't know for sure but we believe you, Jimmy, Lewis, and Carolyn belong to other sets of families. Your father's DNA doesn't match you or your siblings. The only child's DNA that matched anyone in that whole house was Rebecca to Marilyn. Your fathers DNA matches Marilyn's also" Officer Bruce continued.

"Wait, wait, wait a minute" Pa said. "That would make the father and mother related. What do you mean the other children don't belong in this family?" he asked. "That is correct. At this time, we believe that Robert Dingwald is actually Robert Travois, Marilyn's brother. We have not been able to identify Willy yet. Nor have we been able to identify the actual DNA chain for any of the others. That is why we are doing the national DNA testing" Officer Bruce explained. "As for why, I need more information from you Miles. What we need to also figure out is how to deal with all of the theft and if you may have done anything that might cause interference with our theft case against anyone. Rumor has it you and Willy played a major role in how all that stuff ended up at your home. Do you understand what I am asking you?" "Well sort of. I was hoping that my actions would not matter once you saw the rest" he responded. "But I really like the sound of me not supposed to be in this family." Pa laughed and said "I bet you do."

"When we get back to the trailer, Miles and I will need to help the banker with the money and gold. He will calculate total gold value and will actually get a weighted value for us. Our team has finished up in the house and found new evidence that we will have to get answers from Lewis on. Evidently there are more hidden compartments in that house" Officer Bruce explained.

"What kind of information?" Lewis asked. "We found blood on the floor and ropes in a hidden compartment, along with some metal devices that have blood on them. We also found another whip, only it has twice as many nails in it" Officer Bruce told Lewis. "I don't want to talk about any of that!" Lewis responded. "Just leave me alone!" he said. Officer Bruce looked over at Pa and then back at Lewis. "Okay Lewis for now, we will leave you alone" Officer Bruce said.

Once they arrived back at the trailer, Officer Bruce asked one of the other officers to take Lewis back to the station. Officer Green would be expecting him.

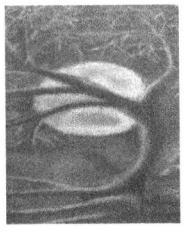

CHAPTER 9- THE TRUTH

They reached the trailer and saw the banker was standing out front talking to Mr. Bufford. Officer Bruce looked up and became quite irritated when he saw him. "Mr. Bufford, to what do we owe the pleasure of your visit?" Officer Bruce asked. "I know Johnny here. He is my banker. I thought I would come over and say hello. Fancy you having someone like him here. You found that pot of gold after all?" Mr. Bufford fishing for answers. "Go away Mr. Bufford" Officer Bruce told him. "If you come back I will arrest you for being a pest." Mr. Bufford dropped his head and walked away. The banker smiled at Officer Bruce. "Thanks" he said. "I am not his banker, he just does his business at my bank. He is terribly nosy if you ask me" Johnny said.

"Johnny, this is Mayor Robinson and this is Miles. Miles and I will help you to access the money and gold. If you would, we need to know how much in weight and actual value there is in the gold and cash. All of it needs to be put into a secure location, so we can protect it until we know where it came from and what the courts will say what to do with it" Officer Bruce explained. "Mayor Robinson, it has been a while" Johnny said. "Mr. Jackson, it is always a pleasure" Pa said. "Mayor, I believe we are working from a first name basis today, will that be okay with you?" Johnny asked. "It will be just fine Johnny" Pa said. "Miles nice to meet you" Johnny stuck out his hand. Miles stuck his out and the older man grabbed his and shook it like he was going to shake it off.

Miles stood there looking at Johnny Jackson, the banker for Little Elm Bank. He was not as tall as Pa and only a little taller than Miles. He figured that made him about five feet three or so. His hair is really dark black and curly, his eyes were brown. His skin was much darker than Miles' was. His left hand had a deformity on it and was missing two fingers. He flashed it at Miles and said it was an old war injury. Miles also noticed he walked with a right leg limp. They turned and Miles and Officer Bruce led Johnny into the house, back into the back room. Miles looked back at him and asked "which one do you want to do first?" "I am sorry?" Johnny looked confused. "Do you want to do the gold or the cash first?" Miles asked.

He looked at Miles and realized he wasn't joking. "Um…the gold I guess" Johnny answered. "What are you going to put the gold in?" Miles asked. "I am sorry, how much are we talking about?" Johnny looked confused. Miles turned around and removed the clothes on the right side to the left side. Then he slid the right back panel to the left. He reached down and pushed the lock, then opened the latch. He turned and opened the box door and moved back. Miles wished he had a camera because the look on that banker's face was priceless. "Can you excuse me for a moment?" Johnny said unnerved. He turned and looked at Officer Bruce "I am going to have to make other provisions for this. I was not expecting this much!" Officer Bruce and Johnny walked back to the front of the house. "You need me to lock this back up?" Miles said with a smile. "Yes please" was the response.

Miles closed and locked the box back up. He walked out to the outside where they were at. Johnny was talking to Pa and Officer Bruce. Johnny then dialed his phone and made a call. Unable to hear what was said on the other end, Miles just listened to the banker make his demands. "I need you to call for a pick up and send it over to this address. I don't care how late it is! I understand that this is not a normal request, but we have a situation that requires our immediate attention! That is correct. I will be here onsite, so tell them they need to make it quick!" Johnny said. "Sorry gentlemen, I was taken off guard by the sheer amount that we need to transport" Johnny said. "You only saw half of it" Miles said. "What?" the banker looked at Miles. "Half?" "Yep" Miles said.

Officer Bruce looked over at Pa and told him "it looks like we are going to be here a while. If you and Miles want to go home, you can take my vehicle and I can catch up with you later." "Naw" Pa said. "We are fine. I gave Ma the keys to the car and you still need to get the rest of the story from Miles." "Why don't we sit down and do that now?" Officer Bruce said.

"Miles" Officer Bruce called him over. "Now is a good time to tell me the rest of your story. I need you to be honest and complete. Understood?" Officer Bruce said. "Understood" Miles answered. "I honestly don't remember where I left off. Where do you want me to start?" he asked.

"How about I just ask you questions and you just answer? I am more concerned that you have not caused us any issues with our current investigations" Officer Bruce said. "Okay" Miles responded. "I am confused as to how we could have caused you issues, when we put the evidence right in front of you" he continued. "When you moved those bodies out of the pond that broke the chain of evidence and you left some of your own evidence there. You say that your mother killed those kids, but you knew where the bodies were and now you are trying to hide the evidence elsewhere. You see how this can get turned around Miles?" Officer Bruce explained.

"Oh, I guess we didn't see it that way. We were just trying to put them closer to the house, so that when you investigated, you would find them. That is why Mr. Bufford came over to let you know where to look" Miles said. "So you involved your neighbor?" Officer Bruce asked. "Of course. We had to plan it out so that we made sure you were able to get what you needed. You guys have been out to this house so many times and never saw or did anything. Even after your officer went out there two nights ago, she still didn't find the bodies. Mr. Bufford was instructed to make sure you knew where to look in the event that you missed them" Miles said. "I see" Officer Bruce responded.

"Do you think you are smarter than the police?" Office Bruce said. "Well…" Miles said in return. "Don't answer that" Officer Bruce said.

"Did you have anyone help you move the bodies?" he asked. "Yes" Miles said. "We paid two of our neighbors those gold bars to help us" he continued. "When you moved the bodies, how did you get them out of the water?" Officer Bruce continued. "Willy and I swam down there and wrapped a plastic bag around the bodies, then tied a rope to them so they could be lifted. Then we pulled them up to the peer, put them into a wheel barrow, and moved them" Miles said. "Why did you wrap them in a plastic bag?" Officer Bruce asked.

"Because I read in a book that you wrote that if a body was submerged in the water, to protect the skin and outer layer of the body by wrapping it with a plastic bag" Miles said. "When did you do all of this?" Officer Bruce asked looking a little confused. "It took us three nights to do it. We would sneak out after everyone was asleep. Then meet them at the tree and go to the pond to get a body. Then we would go back to the tree with the bodies, one at a time" Miles responded.

"If your mom was sneaking out to that tree, how did you keep her from finding out?" Officer Bruce asked. "We covered the ground with leaves and old tree limbs, so she would not see that the ground was disturbed" Miles said. "Okay, let's talk about the stolen goods" Officer Bruce said. What do you know about all of the tools and stuff under the house? What do you know about the watches and jewelry found under the shed? Lastly, what do you know about the stuff down by the river?" Officer Bruce continued.

"I told you I don't know how all of that stuff got under the house. I had nothing to do with any of that and neither did Willy. As for the watches and jewelry, it seems those gold bars came with an added bonus. The two guys we had help us, managed to make that happen. I am not sure where they got them, but one of them did say something about a country club near us. Yes, I know everything about the stuff at the river. Mrs. Rogers owns an old GMC pickup that was broken down. She allowed me to fix it up so that it would run. Willy and I were sneaking out and going to the neighbors' houses across the main road and those people were so stupid. They would just leave this stuff out in their yards and we would just pick it up and move it to the riverbed."

"The dumbass that had that big ass TV, left it next to his house outside leaning on the wall overnight. We just drove by and picked it up and loaded it into the truck. We would sneak out about once or twice every couple of weeks" Miles explained to Officer Bruce.

"You two stole all that stuff with no help?" Officer Bruce asked. "Well, I didn't say that! We had a little help a couple of times. Some of our neighbors are pretty good thieves" Miles said. "No more lies Miles!" Pa said. "Well I didn't lie, I just didn't tell him" Miles said. "Who helped you then?" Pa asked.

"Oh, I can't tell you that. They would get into trouble and I don't want that to happen" Miles said. Officer Bruce looked up at Pa and said "it's okay. I already know who helped them. They didn't do very well with hiding their new found income. They have a new car sitting in their driveway." "A new car?" Miles said. "No way, we only gave them two gold bars!" "How much do you think those bars were worth?" Pa asked. "Hundred dollars" Miles said.

Pa laughed "No, Miles your math is way low. One troy ounce of gold is worth twenty two hundred dollars in today's market. You gave them ten troy ounces."

"No!" said Miles surprised. "That means I paid them twenty two thousand dollars! Holy cow!" "Now there is a priceless look...Miles humbled" Officer Bruce laughed. "Is there anything else you need to tell me? Anything you need me to know?" Officer Bruce asked Miles. "I didn't mean to cause problems with your investigation. I hope we didn't cause an issue with putting them in jail" Miles said.

"I am having a hard time understanding how I could have lived here and at my grandparent's house all this time and not know hardly any of this. Yes, we did a lot of things to try and get you to pay attention, but some of this I know nothing about. The cooker location and that they were doing that stuff. I always thought Rebecca was just being a bitch when she talked about the family business. None of this makes sense at all" Miles confessed.

"Also now that I have told you the truth, what happens to me and Willy?" he asked. "As of right now we have been able to locate the owners of all the items stolen and none of them are pressing charges. They just want their stuff back, except for those that filed insurance claims" Officer Bruce explained.

"The stuff discovered under the house is still being worked out. We actually have reports that go back over twenty years for the stuff we have pulled out of there. The watches and jewelry are still on our list of things to locate the owners for" he continued. "So right now nothing."

"If you think of anything else you need to let me know. I don't believe there will be an issue on getting justice because fortunately we have a good team and we have found a lot of direct evidence that leads back to all three of the suspects" he finished.

"One more thing, I think you are wrong about Lewis and Rebecca. We don't believe they were having sex. Our evidence shows extreme signs of abuse instead. We are going to question Lewis some more today and take him to the hospital to be checked out" Officer Bruce added. "Really?" Miles said. "That sucks!"

Pa looked up and said to Officer Bruce "looks like the money truck is here." "Okay, well I think we have enough for right now. Due to the way you moved the bodies and Lewis' moving the bodies, I believe we will be okay. Let's go get the money gathered up" he said. Officer Bruce looked over at Pa "so, you wrote a book?" Pa said. "Yep" Officer Bruce said.

The truck backed into the driveway, up to the front door. Both of the bank technicians stepped out, looking for Johnny. Johnny came out of the house and greeted them.

"Gentleman, my name is Johnny Jackson. I am the manager of the Little Elm Bank here in town. I need you to bring at least ten boxes and a ledger into the house, so that we can gather up the money and gold bars. When we are done, you will take it all back to my bank. We need to enter all of the gold into the ledger by size and count. I believe the cash is all in one hundred dollar bills. So those need to be counted. Miles, do you know how much is in each packet?" Johnny asked. "No sir, not all of them" Miles said.

"Gentleman, for the purpose of this pickup, let's just count the number of money packages that are in the cabinet and put them into a box" Johnny explained. The two gentleman nodded their heads and went to the back of the truck.

They loaded dollies with at least ten boxes and followed Miles and Johnny to the back room. Once they made it into that second area, they both began unloading each empty box and placing them in the room's corner. Then they opened one box to start the process. Miles turned and asked the question "where do you want to start?" "I am sorry?" the first bank tech said looking a little confused. "Cash or gold, which one?" Miles asked. "Gold" they both responded at the same time.

Miles turned and moved the clothes to the left. Then reached over and pushed against the back panel. He then slid it over to the left. Exposing the steel box. He reached down and pushed the lock until it clicked, unlocking the latch and opening the door to the box. "Huh, that is a lot of gold!" one of the bank tech's said.

Miles watched them as they worked. Johnny logged the amounts into the ledger to help the counting process along, while the other bank employee put the gold into the boxes. Miles felt like he was a security guard watching over these guys, making sure they didn't get sticky hands or try to slip a gold bar into their pockets. It took about an hour and a half to remove all of the gold bars and log them into the ledger.

It turns out there were five ounce bars, one ounce bars, and at the bottom there are five pound bars. Good thing they brought a scale with them as well. Once the log was complete and the boxes were filled, Johnny calculated the actual number of bars for each box and noted it on the bottom. Eighty two one ounce gold bars, sixty one five ounce gold bars, and twelve five pound gold bars.

With the right side now empty, Miles closed the box. He reached over and pulled the back panel back over to the right and moved all the clothes to the right. Now he stepped in front of the left side. He removed the shoes and then placed his fingers into the slot in the back panel and pushed it to the right. He reached down and opened the box on the left side. "Damn!" the other bank tech said. Miles just smiled at his remark.

The bank techs began to go to work. One removes the money packages from the box and handed them over to the other bank tech. He took them out and laid them in stacks of ten each. Once he had enough to fill a box, they stopped and recounted the stacks making sure there were no mistakes. Then all of the packages were placed into the first box. They repeated this process for the rest of the cash. Johnny logged and numbered each box with a number and the estimated total amount of money packages inside each box. No actual total could be calculated for sure until they knew how much was in each package.

Once they were done with loading the money into the boxes, Miles closed the metal box in the closet and they returned to the front of the house where Officer Bruce and Pa were sitting. All of the boxes were scattered around the living room of the house. The bank techs began loading them into their truck outside. Miles stood there thinking about what he could have done with all of that money had she not hidden it. What a waste!

Once all of the boxes were loaded into the bank's truck, Johnny turned and said to Officer Bruce "well...I will get this back to the bank and we will work on getting you a total on everything."

"Would you like me to run research on where this money may have actually come from Officer Bruce?" Johnny asked. "Yes. I was going to talk to you about it later, but since you are here and have asked. We need to see if you can track the money's history and see if we can determine how it ended up here. By legal or illegal means" Officer Bruce responded.

"Pa do we need to go back to the hospital or to your home?" Officer Bruce asked. "I don't actually know" Pa said. "When we left the hospital, Willy was just getting out of surgery and I gave Ma the keys to the car. I need to call her and get an update" Pa said. As Pa made his phone call, Miles looked up at Officer Bruce standing there looking out over the property. "What is on your mind Officer Bruce?" Miles asked him.

"I don't know Miles, but something keeps telling me there is more to find. Maybe not here, but somewhere. You said that Rebecca called this the family business. What did she mean by that?" Officer Bruce asked. "The whole family is in this business" Miles said looking confused.

"What business is that?" Officer Bruce asked again. "Man, it has been enough to just get away from here alive! I am not savvy enough to figure out all the crazy stuff these people are in to! I mean, just today I found out my father is not my father and my brothers and sisters are not my brothers and sisters. How do you expect me to know what kind of crooked business these people are involved in?" Miles responded with anger in his voice.

"Good point" Officer Bruce said. "I don't think I expect you to actually know. I am mostly thinking out loud. For some reason, that one remark leads me to believe we have not found out the core to all of this" Officer Bruce said. "Pa are we ready to go yet? I need to get back to the station and it is getting late. My wife wants me to come home early so I can make it to my son's game" Officer Bruce said.

"Ma is still at the hospital, but if you need to get home you can take us home and I will have Ma drive herself home" Pa said. "If you don't mind" Office Bruce responded. "Can you drive yourself to the house, Ma?" Pa asked her.

"Okay, we will see you there" he finished with Ma and hung up. "She is going to stop and get us some dinner and then meet us at home" Pa told Officer Bruce and Miles.

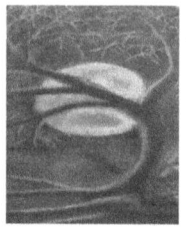

CHAPTER 10- FARMER MILES

They all climbed into Officer Bruce's vehicle and Officer Bruce started the SUV and drove towards the exit of the trailer park. As they began to move, Officer Bruce stopped and began looking out over at the trailer park where all the homes were. He could see Mr. Bufford looking out of his window. Both of the Rogers' boys were watching from their front yard and one other neighbor was mowing his lawn.

Not saying a word Officer Bruce released the brake and took off. As he was leaving the trailer park, he turned back to the left. Driving down the small country road that led to Ma and Pa's house. During the ride, it was absolute silence inside the vehicle.

Once they had arrived, he said "well here we are. I will call you later if any new information arises about the dead bodies or any other evidence, Pa." "Okay" Pa responded. "Thank you for driving us home and let me know how else we can help. Please stay diligent with this and watch for any clues that can provide us more knowledge as to what is really happening. Also, I have been meaning to ask you something but it never seems to be the right time."

"Miles previously mentioned several times that our police department officers have been called out to that park and nothing ever seems to come from these visits. Do you think it might be a good idea to look into this to see what might be going on or if there is any truth to what he is saying?" Pa asked Officer Bruce. "I am way ahead of you. I pulled in one of the City of Paxle's officers and he is going to run an internal investigation for me. I have known him since we were kids and I pretty certain he will be honest with me. Obviously, if I have a problem in my ranks, I need to know" Officer Bruce said. "Sounds good" Pa said. "Let me know what you find out."

Just as Officer Bruce was getting ready to leave Ma pulled into the driveway. "Oh thank God!" thought Miles. I am so hungry! He walked over to her car and helped her get the food out and carry it into the house. Ma sent Miles to wash his hands. Pa came in and after washing his hands, sat down and took a deep breath.

"How is Willy?" he asked Ma. "Oh, he is doing really well. That boy can sure talk your ear off! The surgery went really well and the doctor said he feels like Willy could start walking in a couple of days. If all goes well tonight, the second surgery will be done tomorrow afternoon" Ma said. "Can we go to the hospital?" Miles asked. "Of course" she said. "Pa, do we need to move the horses again tonight and feed the cows?" Miles asked.

"Yes, sir we do" Pa responded. After Miles finished his burger and fries, he got up and told Pa he would meet him at the barn. Pa told him to wait until he got there before he tried to move the horses. "Can I go ahead and put the feed out for the cows?" he asked. "Yes, but remember to check the gate to make sure it is shut first. Don't want any cows eating your hand" Pa said. "Pa, don't tell that boy that!" Ma said. Pa was laughing at himself. "Okay" Miles responded. Miles left the kitchen and went out the back door of the house to the barn.

He got the wheel barrow and pushed it over to the silo where the feed was located. Taking the large bucket, he filled up the wheel barrow as they had done the night before. He picked up the wheel barrow and realized it was much heavier than he expected because it had started to tilt to one side. He tilted it back to stand it up. Getting control, he began to push it. Pa made this look so easy. Miles was determined to feed these cows.

He made his way to the fence line and turned, then thought if I fill the trough first, then ring the bell, that would give me more time to work. So he used the bucket and filled all the troughs with feed, then reached up to ring the bell only to find the rope was much higher than he thought. He climbed up the fence and grabbed the rope. Holding with one hand onto the railing, he pulled the rope with the other hand to ring the bell. He waited at the gate to open it when he saw the cows had arrived. He was just a little proud of himself for a job well done.

About the time he had finished, Pa came out. "Took you long enough" Miles said. "Well, looks like you have it in under control, good job" Pa responded. They pushed the wheel barrow back to the barn and Pa grabbed the harness from the rack. Then as they had done the day before, Pa and Miles went to the pen where the horses were and began moving them to the barn, one at a time. Miles asked Pa "will you ever let these horses get to that girl horse?" "No, we have a stud horse at another ranch that we will bring over here for that" Pa said. "Other ranch?" Miles said. "Yes, our daughter and her husband live across town at our other property. They take care of the rest of our herds" Pa said. "You have more animals?" Miles sounded surprised.

"Yes, we have one hundred and sixty head of cattle, twenty two horses, sixteen sheep, six goats, and about two dozen chickens over at that ranch" Pa said. "We bought that place seven years ago for her and her husband so that we could have our larger farm under their control. We aren't spring chickens anymore, so we need them to be prepared to take over when we are gone." "Where are you going?" Miles asked. "When we die" Pa said. "Oh!" Miles looked surprise. Miles had never heard of anyone talking about when they will die. He had only heard about how they were going to keep from dying.

"As we get older, it gets too hard to keep up with all of this land and animals. My daughter wanted to take over the business" Pa continued. "Why not just give them this place?" Miles asked. "She wanted her own place" he said. "What do you think will happen to the property that we lived in?" Miles asked. "I don't know. It may end up in probate and get sold off by the state" Pa said. "What is probate?" Miles asked. "It is when the courts have to decide who gets what because the owners were not capable or available to make a decision on it" Pa explained. "Will the courts make the decision about all that money?" asked Miles.

"Probably, but it takes years for probate cases to be resolved. I don't think that place will ever be worth anything, you or the others will ever know what happens. We know she owned the property. We will try and get a court judge to rule favorably for the care of all the children that were there. That is a long stretch even with the criminal activity" Pa said. "Most of the time, the family gets the finances or property passed on to them. Since they are looking at jail time and also because of all the damages they have inflicted, it is possible to get a good judge to allow us to push the issue" he continued. "Oh" Miles said. "It's not like anything other than the money is worth worrying about. That trailer home is falling apart and she didn't own much more than the land. At least that's the way it looks right now" Pa said. "That's true" said Miles.

While they were talking, both horses had been moved back into the barn. As they were getting ready to go back to the house, Miles noticed several books on the wall and looked at Pa and asked "can I read those?" "Miles, those are tractor and truck service manuals. Not books for entertainment. If you want to read them I am okay with that, just put them back when you are done" Pa replied.

Excited, Miles looked through them and chose the Model TT service manual first. He pulled it from the shelf and noticed that it was very old and brittle. "Be careful with that one. My great granddaddy got that when he bought the truck. So it is quite old, but still useful" Pa said.

"How long do you think I will stay here?" Miles asked. "Well, Ma and I have talked about this and we have decided to keep you here until the police finish their investigation. Once that is completed, maybe they will turn up something that will help us know what to do" Pa said. "Willy too?" Miles asked. "Yes, Willy too" Pa said. "Thank you" said Miles. "Your welcome" Pa said.

They headed into the house and Miles went back to his room. He placed the book on the bed for him to read later. He took a shower and when he returned to his room, he found both new clothes and another pair of pajamas. He put on the pajamas and climbed into the bed. Excited, he grabbed the Model TT book. As he was getting ready to read, he heard a voice from downstairs. It was Ma coming up the stairs. Miles sat up in the bed to see what was going on.

"Miles" Ma said. "Can you come downstairs for a little bit?" Miles got up out of bed and walked over to the door. He looked down and Ma was standing on the stairs waiting for him. "I am ready for bed Ma and in my pajamas" he said. "That's okay" she said. "I want you to meet someone." "Um…Okay" Miles said, although he was a little nervous about having someone he doesn't know seeing him dressed like this.

He walked down the stairs and Ma started to move towards the hall. As he followed her, his mind began to wonder about who this was she wanted him to meet so late at night. They entered the large room with the fireplace that was bigger than Miles. It was also full of furniture and wood carvings on wood tables. There were huge pictures and paintings on the walls all the way around the room. Sitting inside the room was a woman and two other children. Ma looked back at Miles and said to him "Miles this is my daughter Betty and these are her two babies." "I am not a baby anymore Ma!" the taller one said. Betty turned and gave the child a real stern look.

"The boy is Thomas and the girl is named Mary" Ma said. "It's good to meet you Miles" Betty said. "We wanted to welcome you to the family and let you know you are welcome at our home anytime." "Thank you" Miles said. "How old are the two of you?" Miles asked the two children. "We are both ten, twins actually" Mary responded. "That's how old I am" Miles said.

"Tomorrow, we are going to the hospital in the afternoon to check on Willy and see when they are doing the next surgery on him. In the morning, Pa has to go into work in the early morning hours and I need to go to the school to work also. Would you mind going over to Betty's house and spending the early hours there?" Ma asked Miles. "I am okay with that if they are" Miles said. "Of course" Betty said. "The kids can show you around the farm. We have a few more animals than Mom and Dad do here" she said. "So I have been told" Miles said.

"Well okay then Miles, I guess we will look forward to seeing you in the morning" Betty said. Miles said good bye and went back to his room. He laid down on the bed and thought about the day. He thought about all of his plans to keep everything a lie being blown out of the water. Officer Bruce and Pa know all about what they did now. No more lies to tell. Miles hoped they understood his motives on what made him do all that he did.

He reached over and picked up the service manual to read. His family never understood why he liked to read books like this. He would check books out from the library that were technical. A book this old would not be in the library. So to get the chance to read it was awesome! He opened the book and started with the very first page. One of Miles personal habits was that he would read every word from page one to the last page. He wanted to make sure he didn't miss anything. Not realizing how much time flew by while he had been engaged in reading this book, he discovered that most of the night was over by the time he had finished the last page. So he rolled over and went to sleep. Before he knew it, the sun was in the window.

He rose from the bed and got up to start his day. He changed his clothes and grabbed the book to return it. He headed down to the kitchen to eat. When he got there, Ma was sitting at the table and Pa was not around. "Pa asked if you would feed the pigs and the chickens today" Ma said. "Yeah" Miles said. She reached out to him with something in her hand. "He gave you this so you could cut the bags of feed open. Also he said don't cut yourself" Ma smiled.

Miles took the item. It was Pa's Swiss Army knife. "Cool" Miles said. "What is that?" Ma asked Miles, pointing to the book. "It is one of the service manuals Pa has in the barn. He let me read it last night" Miles answered.

After Miles was finished with breakfast, he went back to his room and put on his boots. Then he went over to the barn and placed the book back on the shelf. He selected the next book on the shelf and found it was for the tractor. He set the book off to the side and then grabbed a bag of feed for the pigs. He moved over to the pen and cut the end of the bag just like he had seen Pa do it. Then he raised the bag over the side of the fence and began to pour it out into the trough. Suddenly the bag began to shift and he was missing the trough. He tried to correct it but the bag was too heavy and almost all of the feed spilled out onto the ground.

Upset by this, Miles tried to salvage what was left. He moved to the second trough and poured the remaining feed into it. He looked back and the pigs didn't care that the food was not in the trough. They were grunting and pushing each other around to eat it. At first he was going to reach in and see if he could pick it up and put it into the trough. But by the way the pigs were shoving each other to get to the feed, he realized that may be a bad idea. He went into the barn and got a rake. He raked the feed out into the pen away from the trough, to allow all the pig's access to it.

Miles placed the rake back into the barn and thought I just won't tell anyone about that. He went over and got a bucket for the chicken feed. Since Pa usually helped, he knew he had to spread feed twice as much as the two of them would have spread. No problem. He began spreading and once he completed that, he stepped back. Farmer Miles he thought, look at me! After putting up the buckets, he grabbed his new book and started towards the house.

Once Miles was back in the house, he went to his room and washed his hands and then changed back into his sneakers. He placed the tractor book on the bed. He walked down the stairs and crossed the house to the kitchen. Just before he entered, he heard Ma say "looking for me?" "Yes, ma'am" he said. "Are you ready to go to Bettie's house?" Ma asked. "Yes ma'am" he said. "Does she work?" Miles asked. "She is a teacher at another school. They won't start back to school for another week" Ma answered. "Let's load up and get moving" Ma said.

Miles followed Ma out to the car and climbed in. Wait…Miles thought, this isn't the same car we drove yesterday. "Miles you can sit up front with me if you like" Ma said. Miles opened the door and climbed out. He walked around to the front passenger side and climbed in. He reached behind him and found the seat belt. "It's over there" Ma said. Miles found it and put it on.

As they were pulling away, Ma could see him looking around the car. "Lose something?" she asked. "Is this a different car?" Miles asked. "Yes, this is my car" Ma said. "You have your own car?" Miles asked now, fully amazed! Ma just laughed and drove off. Not much was said as they drove until Ma looked up and told Miles "Pa told me about all of the stuff you had to do yesterday. How are you feeling about all of this?" Miles had not thought about how he felt about it until now.

"Well" he started. "I hope that they are able to help us. I hope we never have to go back to that house. I hope none of the stuff we did will cause them issues with the arrests. I hope I don't have to go to jail because we stole all of that stuff. Most important, I hope Willy is going to be okay and that he can come be with us. I hope I haven't ruined how you feel about me because I planned things the way I did. I honestly didn't think this through as well as I thought I had."

"Miles, I am just glad you were able to get out of there alive. I don't see how you could think you planned this poorly, when based on everything we know so far, you could not have predicted the outcome. However, you got to where you are was probably the needed path. If we are on it, that just made it easier for you and Willy. As for how I feel, I have always said you are smarter than most of my students, maybe even some of the teachers. I am truly impressed that you were able to hide all of this from me and now here you are" Ma replied.

"I cannot answer all of your questions right now, but I can say that we are committed to helping you and Willy all the way through this. I hope the investigation will come along fairly quickly and we can get some good, honest understanding of everything. We want to know what is going to happen to all of you children, not just the two of you" Ma said to Miles.

Miles had not even thought about Lewis, Jimmy, or Carolyn. He was more worried about him and Willy. Ma turned the car into a dirt drive and began to speed up a hill. As they topped the hill, Miles saw a sight he only dreamed of. The house was huge. A fence line ran all the way down the road with cows and horses lined up all along the side of the road, almost as if they were waiting to greet him.

As they got closer to the house, the chickens were running around everywhere. They were running out in front of the car as fast as they could run. Ma stopped right in front of the house. "Here we are" she said. "My God, it's bigger than your house!" Miles said.

Betty came out the front door and gave her mother a hug. She looked over at Miles and waved her hand up and said "come on in Miles. The others are waiting on you." Miles walked around the car and looked up when Mary came out the door. She came down and grabbed Miles by the hand and said "come on, we are going to the see the goats." Miles looked back at Ma with absolute fear on his face. "Go easy on him Mary, he hasn't been around a farm as much as you" Ma said. "Okay" Mary hollered back at Ma.

Mary was a fast runner and Miles was having an issue keeping up with her. They ran up the stairs into the front door and through at least three rooms before they came out to the back porch. Thomas was waiting on the back porch next to a pool. Thomas joined them and they went out to the field. There were three barns at this house and animals everywhere.

Thomas opened a gate and let the three of them into the third barn. Mary let go of Miles hand and she said "the sheep are over here and the goats live on the other side. We have pens for each of them." "We will go through this pen and then over there" she finished. Thomas opened the gate and held it for them. Mary walked through and looked back.

"Come on" she said. "We won't bite." "It's not you I am worried about" Miles said. "They won't hurt you" Thomas said. Miles stepped into the pen with the sheep. Then they walked across to the other side. He opened the pen for the goats. Miles followed Mary into the pen. "You can pet them if you want to. We tried to ride them, but they got too rough" Mary said. "They won't bite you?" Miles questioned.

Thomas looked at him funny "bite you?" he asked. "What kind of animals do you have where you come from?" Thomas asked. "Raccoons, skunks, and squirrels" Miles said. Of course he was referring to Pa's animals, but they didn't know that.

"So, do you play with the raccoons and skunks?" Thomas asked Miles. "No" he said. Thomas looked at Mary funny and then turned toward the goats. One of them had walked over and Thomas reached outside the pen and got a bucket with some feed. He turned around and took a handful and handed the feed bucket over to Miles. Miles followed his movements and put his hand in the bucket and pulled out a handful as well. Then Mary did the same.

Miles watched as the goats started coming over to them. Thomas put his hand out and the goats started eating the feed right out of his hand. Miles wasn't sure about this but he reached out his hand as far as he could and a goat very softly started licking the food from his hand. It felt kind of funny. He could feel the goat's tongue going up and down on his hand.

The goats did not try to bite him at all, which he liked. The goats were, however, all trying to get to him at once. After about four of them came at him and was trying to get the feed in his hand, Miles grew spooked and threw the remaining feed on the ground. Thomas laughed and said "they get a little feisty when we feed them. You just have to push them back like this." He put his other hand on one of the goat's head and pushed it back. Then the next and the next.

Miles got more feed and tried again. This time he did what Thomas told him to do. As he was playing with Mary and Thomas in the goat pen, he began to wonder how Willy was doing. He hoped that he will get to go to the hospital later on and check on him.

After a short while, Mary said "let's go over to the hay barn and make a fort." Hay barn Miles thought, you have barn with hay in it? Off they went out of the goat pen, running across the yard, to the furthest barn away from the house.

As they approached this barn, Miles was surprised and before he realized it he said "you have a barn full of nothing but hay? Why do you have a barn with nothing but hay?" "So we can feed the cows and horses silly" Mary said. "Pa didn't have a barn with nothing but hay" Miles said. "Yes he does. It's way on the other side of his fields. Pa put it there because all of these cows and horses used to live over there previously" Thomas said. "Oh" said Miles. I guess he hadn't been that far yet.

As they approached the barn, Mary said to Miles "Mom said your Mom was really mean to you." "Yeah, I suppose" Miles responded. "Are you a bad child?" Mary asked. "I don't think I am. Officer Bruce doesn't think I am. Neither does Ma or Pa" Miles responded. They entered the barn and holy molly, Miles thought! It's a barn full of hay! All the way to the top!

"Are you going to come live with us?" Thomas asked. "No, I don't think so. The police are doing an investigation on my mom, dad, and the rest of my family. I don't know where we will end up" Miles said. "Wow! Is there another kid?" Mary asked. "Yes, my brother Willy" Miles said. "He is in the hospital because my brother and mother ran him over with their car" he explained.

"No way!" said Thomas. "Ran him over with the car, man that really sucks! How is he still alive?" he asked. "The doctors said he was lucky" Miles said. "I don't think so. I don't see how being run over with a car can be lucky!" Mary said. "Why did you run away to my grandpa's house?" Mary asked.

"Because we needed help and I knew Ma from school" Miles said. "You are one of her students?" Mary asked. "Yes" Miles said. "Why do you not go to her school?" Miles asked. "We go to private school. Mom said we are advanced for our age, so we need a special school" Mary said. "What does advanced for your age mean?" Miles asked. "We are smarter than all the other kids in regular school. So we have to go to a more advanced school to learn" Thomas said.

Miles thought to himself that he was smarter than all the kids at his school and most of the teachers too! Maybe I should ask for a special school when this is all over. While they were talking, Mary and Thomas had started climbing the piles of hay and headed towards the top. Before Miles knew it, they were almost touching the ceiling. There was an opening just before the top and they are able to climb into it and play. However, it turned out, they .wanted to talk.

"This is cool" Miles said. "We come up here when we don't want to be found. We play hide and seek and Mary sings" Thomas said. "Sings?" Miles asked. Mary looked back and she sat down and started to hum. As she did, Thomas sat down across from her. He loved to listen to his sister sing. She had such a beautiful voice. Then Thomas stood up and walked over to the edge, picked up a guitar and gave it to Mary.

She began to play the guitar and sing a song. Thomas accompanied her on his guitar. Miles had never heard the song, but he really liked it. She had a pretty voice he thought. He never had thought about singing. When she finished, Thomas clapped for her. "You are so good Mary!" he said. "Maybe one day you can sing at Nashville" Mary blushed and put the guitar back to where it was before. "Have you ever rode a horse before?" Mary asked Miles.

"No" Miles answered. "Would you like to?" Thomas asked. "I don't know, is it fun?" Miles asked. "Well, we have these miniature horses that we get to ride. They are lot of fun. We have to ask first" Thomas said. "Let's go Mary, we can saddle one before lunch and he can ride it" Thomas said. All three got up and started climbing back down the hay stack. When they got to the bottom, Mary told Miles "you're a pretty good climber." "Uh, thanks" Miles said.

Once they were all down on the ground, they took off towards the house. As they entered, Mary hollered for their mother. "Mom" she screamed. Mom came running around the corner and saw Mary standing there. "What is it Mary? Everyone okay?" she panicked. "We want to ride the little ponies" Mary said. "They are not little ponies Mary, I have told you that. They are miniatures horses" Mom said.

"I don't care, just keep in mind that Miles is not from a farm, so you need to watch out for him. Some of those horses get a little rowdy. Make sure you pick an easy one" she said.

This was a whole new life Miles thought. They get to play on the farm alone, out there with no one watching over them. He stood there and watched Mary talk to her mother with Thomas standing there picking his nose, waiting on his sister to get permission. Nobody screamed or hit anyone. Thomas grabbed Miles by the arm and said "come on." Miles turned and followed. "She will be out here in a minute. I don't want to sit in there while they argue over those stupid horses name" Thomas said.

"Mom keeps telling us you didn't grow up on a farm. So where did you grow up?" he asked. "We live on Old Robinson Road at the trailer park, back in the woods" Miles said. "There is an Old Robinson Road in Little Elm. Cool, I didn't know we had a road named after Papa" Thomas said. "What kind of house do you have?" he asked. "Trailer" Miles said. "Nothing like this."

Mary came out the door and they took off to the miniature horses. The miniature horses were located up the same dirt road that Ma came down to drop off Miles. Thomas opened the gate and they all went into the area. It was an open field and on the farthest side were these little, short horses. Miles had never seen anything like them before. About eight of them he thought.

Mary told Thomas "would you get the saddle and I will get the harness and blanket?" Thomas nodded and went off to the side of the field to a small barn without a front. They both went inside and she got the harness and blanket and Thomas got the saddle. He looked over at Miles and said "you see that rope, grab it in case we have to chase them." Miles reached up and grabbed the rope.

They walked across the field and the horses began to move away. Thomas dropped the saddle where he was and took the rope from Miles and started putting the loop end above his head, swirling it around and around, and then he took off running towards the horses. The horses got spooked and began running away from him. "Don't spook them!" Mary said. "We have to sneak up on them" she said.

Thomas walked back around the other way and Mary went the opposite. She pointed to Miles to walk in the middle. As they approached the horses, they began to stir but had no direction to run. Thomas walked up to one and placed the rope around its head. "You should be easy enough" he said. They pulled the rope and the horse followed them to where Thomas had dropped the saddle.

Mary placed the blanket on to the horse. Thomas handed Miles the rope and told him to hang on to it. Thomas picked up the saddle and set it on top of the horse. "Make sure you let him breathe first so we can get it the saddle on tight enough" Mary said. "What do you mean breathe?" Miles asked. "When you put the saddle on the horse, they usually take a deep breath, causing them to fill up with air. If you don't let him breathe out first, then when you put the saddle on, the saddle will fall off while you are riding it. We don't want that" Thomas said. "Now that's something we can agree on" Miles said.

While the horse was getting a saddle placed on him by Thomas, Mary began to put the harness on the horse. Once she had it on tight and the bit was in his mouth, she removed the rope. "Okay, Miles. You see this stirrup, put your foot right here. Then you are going to pull yourself up with this saddle horn. Do you want me to show you?" Mary asked. "No, I think I can do it. He is not going to bite me, is he?" Miles said.

"No, but he might jump or move a little when you get on. So hang on tight" Thomas said. Miles placed his left foot into the stirrup and then Thomas put his hand on Miles's butt so that when Miles pulled himself up, Thomas pushed him. Miles's right leg flung around the horse and he landed in saddle. The horse began to squirm and Mary grabbed the reins to hold him in place. Miles got spooked and leaned over and grabbed on tight with both hands.

"You can sit up now" Mary said. Miles began to raise up and sit straight up on the horse. He could only imagine how much work this would be on the bigger horses. "Do you ever ride the bigger horses?" he asked both of them. "Yes we do, only when Dad helps us though" Mary said. Slowly, with Mary holding the reins, she began to walk the horse around in a large circle. Miles was hanging on for dear life.

"Don't be so scared, he is not going to hurt you. I am going to give you the reins because you have to show the horse who is boss" she said. She reached up with the reins and gave them to Miles. "Now, pull back on the reins a little to let the horse know you are in charge" Mary said. Miles pulled back and the horse stopped moving. "Now, give the reins some slack so he will start walking. Don't kick him or he will take off running. When you want to go to the left, pull the reins to the left. Same thing for the right" she continued.

Miles loosened his hold on the reins and the horse started walking forward. He then pulled the reins to the left and the horse started turning to the left. Cool, he thought, this is so easy. He rode the horse around for a while and then Thomas said "do you want to go faster?" "Sure" Miles responded. "Just tap your legs against his back side and he will start to trot." Miles did so and the horse began to take off. However, the instructions on how to stop were not as clear. The horse kept getting faster and faster. Mary was screaming to Miles to pull back on the reins. Miles finally understood what Mary was yelling and pulled back on the reins and the horse began to come to a stop.

Miles' heart was racing a hundred miles a minute. He could feel every beat. Both Mary and Thomas came over with grins from ear to ear. "Was that fun?" Thomas asked. "Want to go again?" Mary asked. "Yes it was fun and no not right now. I think I am done for today" Miles said. He started to climb off the horse but the horse got spooked and took off running with Miles hanging off the side. "Oh shit!" said Thomas. "We have to catch him!" he said. Thomas grabbed the rope. Mary took off to the right and Thomas went left. They chased the horse back against the fence until it stopped running. By now, Miles had pulled himself upright and was back in the saddle. The reins are dragging on the ground.

Thomas, who was in front of the horse, walked right up to him and grabbed the reins. He placed the rope around its neck again. He told Miles "now take your right foot out of the stirrup and slowly put your right leg over the saddle and horse's behind and step off the horse." Miles did as instructed. The horse did not move this time. Once Miles was off the horse, Mary said "my turn." She grabbed the reins and put her foot into the stirrup. Swung her other foot over the horse and into the saddle. She placed her feet back and gave the horse a little kick. Off she went around the field as if nothing had just happened.

Miles, on the other hand, was hoping his heart didn't stop beating. He watched as she rode that horse like an expert. "We might as well go over there and sit down. She will be out there for a while. She loves to ride, especially that horse" Thomas said. Thomas and Miles walked across the field and sat down inside the little barn area. "Your house is really nice. Huge compared to where I live. All of this land and the animals" Miles said.

"How do you feed all of these animals?" Miles asked. "We all work on the farm. I help my dad with the cows and horses. We herd them from that field to this one once every two weeks. Mary helps Mom with the house and we all feed the chickens, goats, and sheep, taking turns. Mary and I are going to join the Four A program next year and show our sheep and goats. We thought about showing a cow, but Dad said it would be a lot more trouble than he felt we would want to do" Thomas told Miles.

"Show, what do you mean?" Miles asked. "The Four A program has a show every year where you take your animals in and they judge them. To see who has the best one. We also have farm vegetables that we will try to win a prize for the best vegetable" Thomas explained.

"Vegetables? You have a farm with vegetables? I thought you just bought them in the store in a bag" Miles said. "Wow, they keep you in a box! You really are sheltered" Thomas said. Miles felt a little stupid about this point.

Mary came over and she asked Thomas if he wanted to ride. Thomas said he did not. She was ready to get off and did. They removed the saddle and hung it back on its rack. Then they removed the blanket and put it on the wall. Lastly, they removed the harness. Miles watched, thinking they both were so smart. They knew exactly what they were doing. Mary reached over and slapped the horse on the butt and he took off towards the rest of the horses.

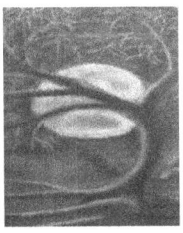

CHAPTER 11- AS TIME GOES ON

Ding, ding, ding rang a bell from the house. "Lunch time" said Mary. All three of the children took off running towards the house, down the dirt road. When they arrived at the house, their mom hollered from inside the house "wipe your feet!" That's when Miles looked down and saw his sneakers covered in dirt and mud or he what he though was mud. Oh man, he thought Ma is going to be so upset! Tears started to well up in his eyes.

Thomas looked over at him and nudged Mary "what's wrong Miles?" she asked. "Ma got me these sneakers a couple of days ago and now there ruined! She is going to be so mad at me" Miles said. "Mom!" Mary hollered. "You need to come out here!" Betty came to the door and saw Miles standing there his eyes watering and she came out the door "what's wrong sweetheart?" she said.

"He said Ma is going to be mad at him because he got his shoes dirty" Mary said. "Well, we can fix that. Take them off and let's put them in the washer and clean them up. What do you say to that?" Mom asked. "Will you do that?" Miles asked. "Of course Miles, it's going to be okay" she said. "My Mom knows you are going to get those sneakers dirty, but if it bothers you, we will take care of them right now" she continued. "Thank you" Miles responded.

Miles removed the shoes and gave them to Betty. The three of them walked into the house towards the kitchen. Miles felt a bit foolish for getting so upset, but if they only knew the truth about why, they would not judge him negatively. As they were about to enter the kitchen, their mom hollered to say "you all need to wash your hands after messing with those horses."

Mary turned and they all headed through the house, down one of the hallways. Mary turned into a room, which Miles later determined was a bathroom. Apparently, it was her bathroom he found out when he tried to enter. "Where do you think you are going?" Mary asked. "To wash my hands" Miles said. "Not in my bathroom you are not! You need to follow Thomas to his bathroom" Mary said. Miles was confused but turned and followed Thomas, who was grinning.

At the table in the kitchen, Miles was looking around the room and the kitchen was really big. The table was not actually in the kitchen. It had a room all to itself. Just like in Ma's house, there are pictures of what looked like the family all over the walls. Also, several cabinets had dishes in them. In the kitchen itself, the counter tops were all clear of any extra stuff on them. In the middle of the kitchen was a stove and oven. Hanging above the stove top were pots and pans. All appliances looked new and had a common copper color on them. The kitchen looked as if it had never been used, it was so clean.

As their mother came back in, Miles heard her say to someone to just make them sandwiches today. Miles would be leaving soon and needed to be ready for when Ma arrived. Miles looked around the corner and there was a lady standing there. "Who is that?" he asked. "Our maid and Nanny" Mary answered. Maid and Nanny Miles thought? How rich are these people? As lunch was being served, Miles heard a familiar voice in the back ground.

It was Ma, she had just returned back from school. She came in and Betty walked into the kitchen and gave her a hug. Ma looked up and said "well, did you guys have a good day together?" "Heck yeah!" Thomas said. "We fed the goats by hand and Miles learned how to ride a horse, well…sort of" Thomas continued. "And we learned about Miles being scared of you!" Mary said. "I am not scared of her!" Miles shot back. "Excuse me, why would you say that Mary?" Ma asked.

"He got his tennis shoes dirty and he thought you would be mad at him" Mary said. "Mom had to wash them" she continued. Ma looked over at Betty with a look of confusion. Instead of getting excited, she said "well first off, as Miles has corrected me, they are not tennis shoes, they are sneakers, right Miles?" Ma said. "Yep" Miles responded. "Second, I see no reason to get upset over a little dirt" Ma said.

"Are we ready to load up and go to the hospital?" Ma asked Miles. "Yes Ma'am" he said. "Can we come too?" Mary asked. "Well maybe next time Mary. Miles' brother is probably going to have to have surgery today and that would be really boring. How about when he gets into rehab you come with us then?" Ma said. Dropping her head and looking up she said "Okay." Betty brought Miles shoes back into the room and handed them over to him. "They look brand new" Betty said. "WOOOO!" Miles said. "Thank you so much."

As Ma and Miles climbed into her car, he looked back at the house these people lived in. He thought about what it must be like to have such big home, with a really nice mother, and all the animals to play with. Most importantly, he thought about not having a big brother always tattling on you and getting you into trouble. Or a mother chasing you down with a whip to beat you.

He continued to think about both Thomas and Mary. All three were about the same height as he was he thought. Thomas had light brown hair and green eyes. His arms were bigger than Miles, probably from working on the farm. Mary had red hair and blue eyes. She had a face full of freckles like Miles. She was skinny and could run fast. Betty, their mother, had a reddish, brown hair and her eyes seemed to be both green and blue. Betty was very pretty Miles thought and not much taller than him.

They have arrived at the hospital and got out of the car to go inside. When they arrived at Willy's room, they found Pa and Office Bruce talking to Willy. Ma and Miles entered Willy's room and Ma asked "how is it going boys?" "Good, just talking with Willy, getting his version of what happened. Doesn't seem to be much different than what we already know" Pa said. "Although he is pleading the fifth on a lot of stuff. Miles did you have anything to do with this?" Pa asked. "What is pleading the fifth?" Miles asked.

"Not telling us anything" Pa said. "Willy, I already told them the truth about what all we did. After I talked to them, we don't want anything we did to stop them from putting the suspects into jail. So just tell the truth" Miles told Willy. "Well, if you told them, why do I need to?" Willy asked. "Because we want to make sure Miles is telling the truth. Your story will confirm his" Officer Bruce said. "Oh" Willy said. "So, now do we need to start over?" Officer Bruce asked. "No" Willy said. "I will tell you what I know."

Pa walked over and took Ma and Miles out of the room. He wanted to let them in on something and needed to be away from Willy to do it. "Bruce has found a family that matches Willy's DNA. An officer has called the family and spoken to Willy's Aunt. She told the calling officer that Willy's parents had separated years ago after their child was taken. Somewhere around nine years ago. The father apparently shot himself and the mother has been in and out of rehab since. She was currently doing well and the Aunt said that she will contact her about Willy. Bruce said they live in a small town in Colorado" Pa said.

"Bruce said they will fly the family out here once they have talked to Willy's mother, if it all matches up" Pa continued. "Oh my God, that is wonderful!" Ma said. "We will see. I cannot imagine the trauma this family had to go through" Pa said. Officer Bruce came out of the room as the nurse was going in. "Looks like we got what we needed. His story seems to mostly to line up with what Miles told us" he said. "Mostly?" Miles responded. "What was different?" he asked. "Something about Mrs. Rogers's boys and some pills" Officer Bruce said. "Oh" Miles smiles. "Not one of my best laid plans" he said.

Pa looked up with a surprised look on his face. "Do we want to know?" he asked Officer Bruce. "Well, it doesn't appear that it ever made it past first base, so I would say no" Officer Bruce said. "Good lord, this whole mess has been such a rollercoaster ride!" Ma said. The nurse came back out and announced to the family that Willy would be taken into surgery in the next half hour, and they could go to the waiting room if they wanted to. Pa looked up and asked "anyone hungry?" "Famished" Ma said.

"I already ate lunch" Miles said. "You can come with us anyway. Willy is going to be in surgery for a while and you won't have anything to do but sit and wait" Pa said. "Maybe, you can fill us in on the pill idea story as well?" Pa continued. "Oh, I don't think I really care" said Ma. "I am so tired of all the terrible things that happened at that house. I feel so bad for all of those children" she continued. As they left the hospital, the nurses were wheeling Willy out of the room for his surgery.

After lunch and a return to the hospital, they sat and waited until the doctor came out. "Well" Dr. Jeffrey said. "Willy's surgery went well. We put a pin in the humorous bone and reset it. I replaced the ball and joint at his shoulder's rotator cuff. The shoulder itself had a small crack in the top of it. I installed a screw there to keep it from coming apart. We put a nontoxic adhesive dressing there as well. It will take a several weeks for all of his bones and joints to heal. Willy's rehab will have to be slow, because we have to heal all of his injuries, including the humorous at the same time. I understand he had hip surgery yesterday and his rehab for it is set to start tomorrow. Today's surgery should not affect that directly, except for the pain and swelling around his injuries" he said.

"Thank you doctor" Pa said. "What is your name?" Pa asked. "I am sorry bad habit, my name is Dr. Jeffrey" the doctor said. "Well, I am Mayor Robinson and this is my wife, Mattie Robinson. This young man is Willy's brother, Miles" Pa explained. Miles thought huh, Mayor Robinson, he never introduces himself as the Mayor. "It's nice to meet you Mr. Mayor" Dr. Jeffrey said.

"How long do you think his rehab will take?" Pa asked. "Well, it just depends on how quickly Willy heals. Normally we only have one break, not two major ones at the same time. However, I would say a couple of week's minimum to get him up and moving. If he is doing well in a couple of days, we will start him moving around to help him heal properly" the doctor explained.

"Can we see him now?" Miles asked. "He will be moved back into his room in a short while. We have him in recovery right now" the doctor responded. "I am going to wait in his room" Miles said. Both Ma and Pa nodded okay. Miles went into Willy's room and sat down to wait for Willy to return. As he sat there, he reviewed the last five days and all the things that had taken place. He will be glad when Willy is better and can come home to Ma and Pa's. After a short wait, Willy was wheeled back in by the nurses, who helped transfer him to his bed. "Oh, hey Miles" Willy said, smiling goofily.

"How do you feel Willy?" Miles asked. "I don't know, but the doctor said I did well. I feel okay, except for being a little sore" Willy said. Pa walked into the room as they were talking. Willy looked up and smiled. "Glad to see you are doing okay" Pa said. "Me too!" Willy said. "I don't ever want to do this again!" he said. "Well, if I have anything to say about it you won't!" Pa remarked. "So when I get out of rehab, will I be coming home with you?" Willy asked. "As of right now, yes you will be" Pa answered.

"Good. Miles tells me you have a really nice house. A lot better than ours" Willy said. "Will I have my own room?" He asked. "Yes you will" Pa said. "You should see his daughter's house" Miles said. "It's even bigger than his and she has a lot more animals!" Miles continued. "So, you liked being over there Miles?" Pa asked. "Yeah, for sure!" Miles responded. "I got to feed the goats by hand and ride a pony" Miles said. "It's is not a pony, it is a miniature horse" Ma said as she walked into the room.

"You need to get you some animals like they have that don't bite!" Miles told Pa. Ma gave Pa a look of confusion, but just let it go. Pa of course laughed. After they visited with Willy for a while, he began to get tired. Willy's speech was slurred and his eyes were drooping. So, they decided to leave and go back to the house, letting Willy rest. It was getting close to dinner time and Ma said she needed to get it started. Once they were home, Miles went to his room and washed his hands. He came back to the kitchen, ready for dinner.

Pa was already sitting at the table and drinking a glass of tea. He looked over at Miles and said "I hear you have already finished that book you got from me yesterday. What did you think?" "Yes, I did. It was awesome! I have read other books on cars and trucks but that one had a lot more information in it. It was like the people that built the truck wanted you to know how to fix it. The newer vehicle books don't help you do that as well" Miles said. "I hope you don't mind, but I got the one to read on the tractor this morning" Miles said. "Not at all. Maybe you can work on that old tractor for me" Pa responded.

Each day, Miles and Ma would go up to the hospital and check on Willy. Before they left the house, Miles had a set of chores he was expected to get done. He had to feed the cows, pigs, and chickens and then Pa would help him feed the horses. The female horse was taken away to the other farm, so she was not an issue anymore. Some nights, Pa put all of his horses out into the fields and left them there overnight.

School was back in session and Miles had to go to school before they could go to the hospital. Miles and Ma tried to go to visit Willy every day in the afternoon after school, when he had rehab. Pa was working all day as a Mayor and normally came home later in the evening. Miles usually had to take care of the cows by the time he got home. In the morning, they both got up and fed the chickens and pigs. Some days, Miles did all of the animal feeding by himself.

Time passed as Willy healed and was getting closer to coming home. Miles couldn't wait for his brother to see his new home! It had been three weeks since the surgeries. He was still unable to walk without a walker or crutches. Although last week, he was able to stand and not fall over. He was putting weight on his injured leg every day. He also had full movement in his arm, but still had a problem lifting it. The doctors gave Ma a list of exercises Willy needed to continue doing once he arrived home. She had hired a personal trainer, qualified to help him continue his physical therapy at home.

Miles had not heard anything more about his own family or the investigation and he was not asking. Miles never had a home like this or a family that treated him so nice. On the weekends, he got to go over to Betty's house and play with Thomas and Mary. Last weekend, a goat got out of the pen and they had to chase it down. That sucker was fast! Thomas and Mary trapped it in the fencing's corner. Thomas had Miles put the rope on the goat and pull him back to the goat pen. It was fun Miles thought.

"Miles" Pa called him over. One of Miles chores he had to do when Pa was not around was to move hay into the barn in each horse stall. But first he had to muck out each horse stall which meant getting rid of older straw that had horse poop and pee in it. Yuck! Not his favorite chore. Then using a pitch fork, he would carry the new hay in and place it in each of the stalls. Of course, no horses were in the stall when he did this.

After that chore was completed Miles would stop and walk up to the house. Pa laughed at Miles because he had his boots on with his pants shoved into the top of the boots, like he had seen Thomas wear his pants. "You look like a real cowboy now" Pa said. "I think we need to get you a real cowboy hat."

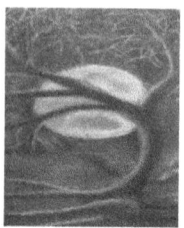

CHAPTER 12- THE SURPRISE

"Officer Bruce has asked that we come to the station today so we can get an update on the status of the investigation. So you need to come in and clean up. You can do the rest later" Pa said. Without saying a word, Miles put the pitch fork up and closed up the stalls. Hethen closed the barn and went up to the house. As he went into the house, he heard Ma say "wipe those feet off." Miles grinned because that's the same thing Betty said to them when they are going into her house.

Once Miles was cleaned up, Ma had made a small lunch for them to eat. They loaded up into the car and started going to the police station. "Did he say what he wanted to talk about?" Miles asked. "He said they had been doing an exhausting investigation and would just like for us to know where everything was at" Pa said. "Oh, okay" Miles responded. Miles watched out the window at the scenery as they traveled. Over the past three weeks he had become quite familiar with this area.

As they arrived at the police station, Miles stomach got a little queasy. He was afraid that this was the end of the line. His good fortune was about to be over. Officer Bruce had found out who his and Willy's real family were and they would be taken away to some far away land no one knew about. To live with families they didn't know. They got out of the car and as they were going inside the police station, Miles stopped. He looked at Ma and said "I don't want to go in. I am afraid he is going to take me away from you and Pa."

"Well, I understand your concern Miles" Ma said. "Wouldn't you want to know who your real parents are? Who your mother and father really are or if you actually have real sisters and brothers? To know who those people were that you were taken from? They deserve to know the truth and so do you" she said. "Yeah" Miles said. "But I like being with you and Pa. I don't want to lose what I have here. If my real parents wanted me that bad don't you think they would have a came and got me by now?" Miles said almost in tears.

"I don't know if that is a fair question Miles. I understand what you are saying but I promise you we will not let you go anywhere that we are not sure is in your best interests. Okay?" she said to Miles. Miles just turned and started walking towards the police department's door. As they entered, the person at the desk came to the front and told them to follow him. They walked through the police station and turned into a large room full of police and several plains clothes officers. Miles noticed Federal Bureau of Investigations (FBI) badges on at least three of them.

"Good afternoon. Now that Mayor Robinson and his family is here, we can get started" Officer Bruce announced. "As you were aware a few weeks ago everything that was involved in this investigation was from a local level. As you can see around this room, things have changed and we have invested a massive amount of hours and people to make all of what you are about to hear happen. To begin today, we have fourteen other locations on the screen that are listening in. Do all of you have visuals at this time? Okay, good. Looks like we are ready to roll" Officer Bruce said as he sat up front and looked at Ma and Pa.

"I would ask that you let me go through this before you ask any questions. There is a lot to cover and a lot to explain. I realize you have questions and were expecting me to give you a one on one update. However since the last time we were together, the investigation has taken a big turn about a two weeks ago."

"As for our local group, we can cover some of that first. All the items we found that were stolen, from under the trailer to the items we found outside the home, have been returned to the original owners. As for Willy and Miles involvement, I will discuss that with you and Ma after we finish here today. Most of the owners were just happy to get their stuff back. As for the watches and the jewelry, they have been a little harder to find the actual owners. None of that stuff was turned in as stolen" Officer Miles begins his presentation.

"When our investigation began, it included a small family here in Little Elm at a trailer park. Since then, it has branched out to fifteen other locations. What we have discovered is a nationwide child trafficking ring. An entire family has been stealing babies and children for the better part of the last thirty years and selling them on the black market. It appears the thefts started in Grandville, Texas with the grandmother and grandfather."

"As time has gone by, the family network has branched out to over thirty states with sixteen total locations. So if you ask how they can be in thirty states and only have sixteen locations it is because the family has scouts that were going out when needed to find more children and abduct them. These scouts crossed state lines and brought the children back to their home bases."

"Once a child was taken to a location, which was generally remote, they are kept there until a buyer was found. According to our investigation, each group tried to sell each child within a year of their abduction. If they didn't sell them, then the child was moved to a new location to stay until a family member until a buyer was found within a year from their abduction. When a child reached a certain age, they came here to Little Elm to be disposed of.

It appears the mother kept the children until they reached twelve and if she has not found a buyer, she executed them and disposed of their bodies. As harsh as this may sound, it is what we have found out about their operations. So we need to get prepared for what comes next."

"If you look around the room, you will see FBI agents, as well as Federal CPS officers. We've been asked to help them initiate their operations because time is essential for all of these children. Once word gets out that we have found their sixteen locations sites, we are certain they will start packing up and moving. So we need to act quickly."

"Three major things have taken place so far. One, the mother, her daughter and father/brother have been confined to special facilities that will prevent them from talking to each other or anyone else in their family. We had to get gag order on their lawyers and anyone else involved in this case. We have located and arrested the grandparents in Grandville, Texas. That particular arrest brought with it a surprise documentation trail that showed every child they had sold previously and who had bought them."

"The warrant that was acquired, allowed us to perform a thorough investigation of the entire facility. We found an underground bunker that held all of these documents. It also provided us with the information we needed to find the other locations. Special thanks go to the Texas State Law Enforcement for their diligence in acting quickly to raid that site. Today, we will be raiding the remaining fourteen locations viewed here online. We are connected to all the local law enforcements that are awaiting for the 'go' command. Ma and Pa, we invited you here because we felt you would want to see what was happening."

"After the raid is complete, we will discuss the rest of the information we have concerning the children here in Little Elm. Miles you are about to be a national hero, son. Officer Green is everyone ready?" Officer Bruce said. "Yes" Officer Green confirmed. "Then we are a GO!" Officer Bruce announced.

Miles looked over at Pa "what is going on?" he asked. "Watch the screen. They are arresting the families at fourteen more locations. Not just here, but all around the country. Look at all those children! Their lives have been saved because you stood up and fought back Miles!" Pa said. "This criminal family will never see the light of day again! They will be incarcerated for life!" Pa continued. As they watched the screen, Miles could not believe how many children there were. Right in front of everyone. There must be over one hundred children of all ages.

After what seemed like hours, Officer Bruce stepped back to the podium. He looked around the room and at the monitor. "All of you should be proud of yourselves today. I realize this has been a tough road, but in a short time we learned a lot about what people were capable of doing with this investigation."

"We saved the lives of every single child you just saw! We also identified all of the scouts and they were arrested this morning as well. On top of this, we have been able to identify the buyers of the children that were sold also, so we can follow those up and arrest them as well and get those children back to their own families" Officer Bruce announced.

"I am not sure how far back in time we will be able to go. Whether or not we can locate all of the children or adults that were taken years ago. We have the authorization to follow this all the way through."

"Let's not forget the hero in all of this, Miles! If he had not stepped up and pushed back locally, none of this would have ever happened!" Officer Bruce said. The room turned and looked at Miles. "Oh no, I am no hero. I was just trying to stay alive. All the stuff we did had nothing to do with all those other kids. As happy as I am that you were able to find them, I am more excited to no longer be living there with that family! Man, I just wanted out alive! I hope you can find these other children's families" Miles said.

Officer Bruce continued his announcements "so, let's talk a little about how the financing of this little network worked. We believe that today the mother here locally was financing the other locations to start with, then when they began to sell their kidnapped children, they would take care of financing themselves. It turns out, the gold that was collected here at the trailer park was bought legally. We believe it was purchased with money from these children, which in turn should make it illegal. The father/brother moved here from Grandville, Texas after the business here started. He invested the proceeds from the business into gold bars back in the late sixties at a very low cost. He had a degree in finance and was an investor on the side."

"What we have determined is that Marilyn's father and mother were brother and sister also. They had two children. Marilyn Travois and Roger Travois. Roger called himself Robert Dingwald, who he got the name from the real financial manager that his father bought the gold from" Officer Bruce continued.

"Roger took the real Robert Dingwald's name when Marilyn and he decided to kill the real Robert Dingwald for unknown reasons. Rebecca is Roger and Marilyn's offspring. Rebecca was their only child. Which by the way, we had originally been told Rebecca was fourteen. That is incorrect. She is twenty eight years of age" Officer Bruce said.

The one hundred dollar bills were the proceeds from the loans and interest paid back by the locations. We expect to find more cash at the other locations now that we have started the raids. We won't know for a few weeks. We have discussed the local money/gold and think we are going to try and push for the courts to release that money for use to use to help all of these children. They will need a lot of help" he continued. "I realize this came together really fast. You can thank all of the people in this room and all around the country for their tireless work that has been put in to reach this point."

"On a local level, we have been interviewing all of the family members, along with their neighbors, to try and gather as much information as we can. After an intense interview with Marilyn, we determined she was not willing to be helpful in any way. Her lawyer is working to get her off because the bodies were moved from the original location. However, we found several other crimes she is suspected on to keep her locked up. It appears that Jimmy had been playing a role to keep from being put into the pond or cooked at the cooker" Officer Bruce explained.

"It turns out he was quite talkative. Jimmy found out that if he played the bad boy tattler and made her think he was on her side, she wouldn't get rid of him. He did apologize for hurting Willy but felt he had to play the role or get killed. After all that I have seen, I can understand his position, though I do not agree with his actions. He said he knew about Miles and Willy's plans and decided to play along, maybe even help" Office Bruce explained.

"He acquired a camera, which he used when they were drowning a child in the pond or sacrificing them at the cooker. They did not know he was there and that he had filmed their actions. I have seen the footage and it's really horrible! Her lawyers are fighting the videos as we speak. I don't believe the judge will find for her once he sees what is on those videos. If he does, we still have Jimmy's witness testimony" office Bruce continued.

"We are currently holding Jimmy in a Juvenile Detention Center. He will still be charged for what he did to Willy, but not as an adult. He was also sent to a counselor for evaluation. It was found that, other than needing help to process all of his trauma, he was not mentally ill. It will be highly recommended in court that he be placed in a mental facility and provided with more help" he continued.

We were able to get a DNA match on Jimmy and his parents and have contacted them. His family lives in North Dakota. They are as ecstatic as one can imagine. They are sending in a DNA sample for comparison testing to make sure it matches before they fly out here. He was taken from them when he was three. They live near a park with their three other children. Jimmy was playing in the sand box and the mother was only a few feet away. She turned around when one of the other children had fallen and went to help them. She said she was only gone for a few seconds and Jimmy was gone. His real name is Jeffrey.

"We interviewed Rebecca and Roger and it turns out they have been dying to get Marilyn out of there for some time. Both of them rolled on her like a Mack truck. Rebecca has phone footage showing Marilyn performing a sacrifice on the last boy she disposed of. I believe his name was Tim. We are trying to identify the other people in the cooker from the pictures and the bones. So far with very little luck" as Officer Bruce stops to catch his breath. "Lewis told us Rebecca performed the sacrifice on that boy herself. However, the footage she has tells another story".

"Roger had decided that Marilyn had gone too far and wanted her out as well. So he has been gathering information and pictures showing her at the pond, drowning the children, and at home locking them into the shed. Roger had installed two field cameras. Both have video and photo capabilities. He pulled all of the cards and saved them. We have five years' of sim cards that we are going through to see what videos and photos are very damning and extremely hard to watch. How about we stop for a little while, take a break, and come back in thirty minutes?" Officer Bruce suggests.

Miles felt like he had entered wonderland, as he sat there watching all of the information come in. He never knew Jimmy was on his side. He always thought he was against him. He also wondered why a.k.a. Dad and Rebecca did not just kill Marilyn if they wanted her out. He looked over at Ma and she had tears in her eyes. "Why are you crying Ma?" Miles asked. "It's all so sad. Just so overwhelming to watch all those children and adults go through this" she said. "I just don't see how you did it Miles" Ma said to him. "I had to" Miles said.

Officer Bruce came back to the front and announced that he was ready to resume his briefing. "Alright, let's come back and get started. I know most of you would like to get back to work. It appears the owner of the watches and jewelry have been located. He will be coming in later today to identify and pick them up. He wants to give Miles a reward for returning them" Officer Bruce said. "Maybe I should do this more often" Miles popped off, as the room full of officers all busted out in laughter. "How about we not and say we did?" Pa said.

"Where was I, oh yes, the next person on the list is Lewis. It appears that our original information on Lewis was completely false. Neither he nor Rebecca admit to having a relationship other than the one provided by the mother. Which included a large amount of very disturbing abuse to Lewis. Each night Rebecca would perform some satanic rituals on him, which included everything from probes in the nether regions to hogtying him up like a calf. We found other extreme body insertions as well. Alleged charges for child abuse, extreme abuse to a minor, illegal sexual abuse of a minor, all have been added to Rebecca's offences" he continued.

"Lewis is currently being held with CPS and we have matched his DNA to a family in Georgia. We have contacted the family and his mother and father are willing to provide DNA samples to verify that they are truly his parents" Officer Bruce explained. "Lewis is fourteen years old and according to his parents he was stolen when he was two" he explained. "The father said that they were at a fair ground walking around. Lewis was in a child stroller and he said his wife had stopped at a small shop. He had walked over to a knife shop while she was in the other shop where she had Lewis with her. She turned around and the stroller was gone. She has never forgiven herself for that. His real name is Larry."

"The next child is Carolyn and since she is the youngest, we spent time gathering DNA from her and searching national databases. We found her DNA in several places across the country. It turns out her actual parents are from Canada. We were able to contact a family member, who turned out to be her Uncle James. James gave us Carolyn's mother's number but we have not been able to reach her yet. Hopefully, she will return our calls soon" Officer Bruce continued with updates.

"DNA matches have been extremely helpful in this process. Getting family members to share their DNA has helped us to tie these children to their families. Yes, we have been able to use various DNA companies as helpful tools to locate some of these families. The local courts were able to give us that authority. I am sure when the FBI and other law enforcements around the country are ready to start, they will use them as well. Our last two children on a local level are Willy and Miles. Willy has been linked to a family in Colorado" Officer Bruce taking a deep breath.

"His mother returned our call and according to her Willy disappeared while in his stroller when he was one years old. It has really taken a toll on the family. The father committed suicide and the mother has been in and out of rehab. She is currently doing well. Which I can only imagine how hard this can be. The mother's name is Barbara Combs. Willy's real name is William Combs. He was named after her father. She is set to arrive tonight, and we will need to pick her up.

Officer Rice can you help with that?" He requested. "Of course" she said. "She did not want to send in a DNA sample in advance" Officer Bruce said. "We will have accommodations set up at the Hilton across from the police station for all of the families. The war room has the flight information for you" Officer Bruce told Officer Rice. "Okay" she said.

"One more thing, before we talk about Miles' DNA matches. It was brought to my attention that our officers had been called out to this location many times over the years and that they did not notice any foul play or other illegal activities. I had the City of Paxle send in two officers to do an investigation. The results of which were very pleasing to me, but maybe not so much for Miles or the family. It turns out the phone number that had been used to call the police was not to the police department. Instead two gentlemen, whom are arrested now, were pretending to be officers that answered those calls. According to all the neighbors, Marilyn had provided them with a phone number that she said was to a special branch of the local police force in case there was an emergency at her house."

"Mr. Bufford told our officers that the last time he called the police was a few weeks ago. That's when he realized that there had to be something wrong with that number. So he looked up the main line and called it. That's when we actually made our first and only official police visit. I realize that we were still remiss for not doing a better job of looking around at that time either. Which is why we are going to set a task force together here locally to try and make sure we do a better job. If nothing else we realized we need to improve."

"Okay...last but not least Mr. Miles" Officer Bruce paused. Miles had been sitting, trying to grasp all of what he was hearing. However, it was not making much sense. Grand Ville, Texas not Grandview, Texas. None of his family was his family. Grandparents that were not grandparents. His brothers and sister, none were real. Jimmy helping him, instead of hurting him. Marilyn's brother being Roger instead of Robert and not her husband. Roger/Robert had also been trying to help him.

Everything he thought he knew was wrong. So many lies! Everything he planned had no bearing on anything. Now he was about to find out whether he too had a family he had never met. All of this was so confusing. He knew that he had been in that house for at least a couple of years.

What happened to all the years before? Who were these people? Why me, he thought. As he sat there wondering, Miles reached into his pocket and pulled out the coin that Rebecca threw at him when he was eight years old. She told him it was his and that he would never see them again. See who again he thought. It was a pin but the back was broken off somewhere during its lifespan. He kept it, not knowing why.

Miles flipped it over and looked at it. On the front of the coin was a carving of three baby's heads next to each other. Underneath the inscribed words were 'Collins Three'. Ma looked down and saw it and said "where did you get that Miles?" she asked. "Rebecca gave it to me when I moved here. She said it belonged to my family and it was pinned to me as a baby" Miles said. "I just figured she was lying. I don't know why I have kept it all these years. Maybe I just wished it was true."

Ma took the coin and stood up. Her eyes full of tears and she let out a scream "OH MY GOD, IT'S MICHAEL!" she screamed so loud it could be heard at the front desk. You could hear the cracking in her voice. As she stood there with her tears falling down her face, she went to her knees crying as if she had just been told someone died. "IT'S MICHAEL!" she repeated. Crying and bowing her head down to her knees. Pa looked up and squatted next to his wife. "What are you talking about?" he asked. She handed him the coin. Pa fell backwards onto a chair, almost hitting the ground. At this point Officer Bruce said "oh my God! I had forgotten all about that. That explains it! Officer Green go get me the file on Michael Collins. It's on my desk."

Pa reached into his pocket and called Betty. "You and Jake need to get up here to the police station right now! I don't care what you are doing, NOW!" he announced. Officer Bruce came over and said to Pa "I am so sorry I did not connect the dots. Our testing kept coming back to you, but I couldn't make any sense of it" Officer Bruce said to Pa.

"How could this happen? Our own grandbaby stolen right from under our noses and living right down the street all this time! Hell, I am his teacher for God's sake! How can this happen right in plain sight and we had no idea about it?" Ma emotionally exclaimed. "I don't know" Pa said.

"I can answer that one" Miles said. "I spoke to one of my neighbors, I think you will recognize his name as Roberto Cortez" he said. "The leader of the drug cartel in Mexico. You spoke to him at your trailer park?" an officer for the FBI said. "Yes" Miles responded. "You see, he said the cartel had lost control of its local business and a whole host of new people were coming in to take over control" Miles continued to share.

"The drug business he ran was getting out of control. Killing people for no reasons every day. Causing major chaos. So he decided to move out and let the crazies just kill each other off and when it calmed down he will go back. He said the best and smartest criminals or bad people hide in plain sight" he continued to talk.

"Most people know they are there but do nothing. They turn their backs and look the other way, mostly for fear they will get hurt. He never did business in this town he said, but he ran his business out of this town. Everybody knows it but no one says anything. Hidden in plain sight he said, that's the best business decision he had ever made."

"He also said it was the greatest flaw in law enforcement because they were always looking for external cracks, disregarding what was right in front of them. He offered to take care of Marilyn for me and Willy, but I told him no. People don't deserve to die, no matter who they are" Miles said.

The whole room was now at a standstill. Not one word was spoken. Ma was still crying and Pa was still sitting there, completely stunned. Miles, on the other hand, was confused. "I didn't mean to upset you Ma" he said. "Oh my God son, you did not make me mad! You just gave me the greatest gift of my life!" she said as she stared at him. "Officer Bruce, what percent of that DNA matched Pa and I?" she asked.

"Pa's match was at eighty two percent and yours was at eighty five percent. We thought it was a mistake and tested it at three different facilities. I was getting ready to pay a company to run it a fourth time. I am sorry I had forgotten about Michael and his case" Officer Bruce said.

Officer Green returned and gave Officer Bruce the file. He took it over and opened it up. Inside was a huge amount of evidence that never led to any results. Officer Bruce wanted to see if anything in that file would have led them to Miles earlier. As he went through the folder, he found a picture and in the background of the picture was Marilyn staring at the camera smiling.

Just standing there smoking a cigarette with a baby stroller. "Oh my God!" he said. "She was standing there with Michael taunting us! I bet she had him in that stroller while we were all searching everywhere for him!" Officer Bruce said. "Hidden in plain sight, I cannot believe this!" he said.

"Okay, now I am confused" Miles said. "Who is Michael and what is going on?" Just as he asked the question Betty and Jake came in the door. "Mom are you okay? Why are you on the floor? Dad, what is going on?" Betty asked. Ma took a deep breath and she reached over and grabbed Pa's hand. "Help me up" she said. Pa helped her lift herself off the ground and he stood up with her. "Bruce" Pa said. "Let's get them tested right away. The sooner we know for sure, the better" Pa told Officer Bruce. "Yes sir" he said.

"You need to let them give you a DNA test. We think that Miles is Michael!" Ma said. Tears welled up in Betty and Jakes eyes. For years they have spent thousands of dollars on detectives and special private investigators trying to locate him. "We don't need to be tested. We have all been DNA tested at our house and we have the results on my phone" Betty explained.

As she fumbled for her phone, Officer Bruce said "we can use your information today but we will need to do an actual confirmation test as well." "I spent three thousand dollars on this test last month. Is that confirmation enough for you?" Betty said. Her hands were shaking so badly she couldn't open the phone. Jake took it from her and put in her code.

Officer Bruce looked at Pa and said "can you help me here?" he asked. "Let's just see what she has for today. We will do a comparison DNA analysis through one of the state's companies later. If she has results, then your tech can do a local comparison and see what it says" Pa said. Betty was standing with tears pouring out of her eyes. She was so shook up, she could hardly stand. Pa walked over and put his arm around her.

Once Betty's phone was opened, Jake opened the app that had the DNA results. He handed the phone over to Officer Bruce and he walked away with it. Now Miles was starting to get it. "So, I am not Miles Dingwald? If this DNA matches what mine is then I am Michael Collins your son? Which means I get to live in the big house with all the animals?" Miles said. "I have a twin brother and sister?" Yes" Betty said. "I had triplets" she said. "You are our third child!" she said just as she busted into tears.

"Well, I don't know why you are crying Mrs. Betty, but this could be the happiest day of my life! So don't pay me no mind if I do a little happy dance!" Miles said. "You go right ahead" Pa said. "I think you have earned it." They waited in the room, not noticing that all of the officers and FBI officers were still just sitting there, waiting for the results. A good ending to terrible ordeal.

Officer Bruce came back with a really big smile. He handed the phone back to Jake and said "my tech said your DNA testing is an exact match to you and your husband. Miles is Michael Collins. Also, we were able to print the report off of your phone, so no more testing will be needed" Officer Bruce said. Betty reached over and grabbed Michael up like he was a rag doll. She hugged him so hard Michael thought he was going to break.

"So what happens now?" Pa asked Officer Bruce. "For today, you take your grandson home. I will come and see all of you later, when I understand what will happen to Miles, I mean Michael, for the theft and other things he was involved in. We have a whole nation of locations that we will be assisting over the next several months. So I am uncertain as to when I will be able to follow up again with you all. In the meantime, I am going to put a task force together to try and find a solution to the hiding in plain sight issue."

"This really has opened my eyes, even though we had a positive outcome today. There were twenty or maybe even more years behind us that we did not know about. So many children and so many lives we missed because we didn't pay attention" Officer Bruce said shaking his head.

"I will be over here tomorrow. I want to be on that task force" Pa said. "Me too" Michael said. "Yes sir" Officer Bruce responded. As they started to walk out of the police station, Michael stopped and turned back to Officer Bruce. He walked over to him and reached out and put his arms around his waist giving him a big hug. Officer Bruce just looked down and patted him on the head. "Thank you so much for helping and believing in me" Michael said.

"Well now, I can say the same to you. Thank you for your help and for believing in us. Maybe one day when you grow up you will come work for us" he said in return.

Michael turned around and walked over to Betty and Jake. He reached up and took each of their hands as they walked out the door. Ma and Pa were right behind them, holding hands. "Pa can we go by the trailer park on the way back home? I just remembered somethings I need to give to Officer Bruce on this case" he asked.

"Don't ask me, ask your mom" Pa said. "Cool" Michael said. "Mom" he said with a smile "what is it we need to go get?" Mom asked. "I may have taken a little more of that gold than I originally said. Also, a small book that she had that may show how she spent the money. It's buried in the ground in the woods. I want to go get the gold and give it to Officer Bruce so he can help the other kids" Michael said. Pa just smiled and looked at Betty "I know, he is your son."

Betty stopped walking and turned and looked at Pa. "I assume you will give us an update on what he is talking about" she said. "Just ask him. I bet he will be happy to tell you the whole story" Pa said. She turned and looked at Michael and he said "Do you want me to tell you now?" "How about we go by the house to get what you left and then we will go home, then you can give us an update then?" Jake said. At that point Michael realized Jake was his father. He smiled and said "okay."

Michael looked over at Pa and Ma and smiled. "I am sure glad this turned out the way it did! I wasn't looking forward to meeting new people." "Me too!" said Ma. Betty just looked at Michael and smiled. Jake held his hand as they were getting ready to get into their car. "Pa?" Michael asked "what do you think will happen to me?" "How about we just get through today and we will worry about that when it happens?" Pa said. "Okay" Michael responded.

As they left the police station, Michael rode in the back seat with his father driving and mother on the passenger side. Michael thought about his new name, his new home, and having his own room. Maybe even his own bathroom. Getting to play with Thomas and Mary every day. Betty looked at him and said "I missed you so much and I love you with all my heart!" Oh my… Michael thought! He had never heard those words before. Tears welled up in his eyes as he took in how he felt about it all.

…And then…

Preface

"Michael, Michael, Michael, over and over again he repeated this name in his mind. All those years being known as Miles have been engrained into his into his brain and every time his mother or siblings called his name he never heard them until they call him by his other name. His mother Betty has asked him repeatedly why he cannot remember his name. 'Why is it when I call you Miles you respond? You need to forget that name and respond when I call you Michael' she will say. All his life Miles was his name and now suddenly everything has changed. He has a new home, his own room, his own bathroom. He has plenty of clothes and two pairs of sneakers instead of one. He gets to play with Thomas and Mary on the farm. He gets to ride the horses and feed the goats and sometime just go off and play by himself. All the things he ever dreamed of are at his disposal and he can't remember his own name. He cannot understand why he is having so much trouble after six months he thought he would have this problem solved, but something inside him is questioning his existence. Something he cannot seem to understand. Why it is all this wonderful stuff surrounds him and he cannot enjoy it.

About the Author

Mark has spent the vast majority of his life, dreaming, and wanting to share his creativity and inventive nature with the world. Lies Unseen is Mark's first attempt at sharing himself through the joy of fictional writing. Mark lives with his wife, domestic cats, and numerous critters in their back yard.